SIXTEEN YEARS
to
LIFE

Jamie Morrison

PAPERBACK ISBN: 9798988871699

HARDBACK ISBN: 9798988871675

Jamiejai.com

Third Edition

To my mother, thank you for your strength, love, and support.

Truly soul of my soul.

Ava and Phoenix, flesh of my flesh, bone of my bone. Thanks for making me a mother. Your hugs, kisses, and laughter made it all worth it. I love you both with all my heart and soul.

Table of Contents

PART III
NO ONE TOLD ME I WAS GROWING UP

PART IV
WHAT I CARRIED IN SILENCE

PREFACE

SIXTEEN YEARS TO LIFE. That was her sentence. My mother went to prison without warning. One day she was there, laughing, brushing my sister's hair, kissing my baby brother's toes, and the next, she was just gone. Not in the way people go to work, run errands, or even leave for a while - she was gone in the way that tears something from your chest, leaves a cold echo where a warm body used to be.

I was twelve years old. My sister was six. My baby brother was just six months. It was the end of summer, the Texas air heavy and still as if it knew something we didn't. School was just weeks away. I was supposed to be excited about starting middle school. My mother always made the back-to-school season feel special, taking pride in getting us new outfits, fresh sneakers, colorful notebooks, and the perfect backpack. Even when money was tight, she made magic out of nothing. She always did.

That summer, she smiled more than usual. She held us closer. We piled into her bed, danced in the living room, and stayed up late watching movies. I thought it was just a good summer. Now, I know it was our last one we'd spend together with her as children.

In those final weeks, she and my grandmother started waking up early, dressing in their best suits, and leaving for hours. I didn't ask where they were going. I just watched them leave, saw the worry in their eyes grow deeper each day. Then came the night I'll never forget.

I heard my mother crying. It wasn't the kind of cry you do when you stub your toe or watch a sad movie. This was crying that breaks the silence of the house, the kind your spirit can feel. She was praying too, words tumbling out in a whisper, shaking with desperation. I didn't know what she was asking God for but I followed her, barefoot and quiet, imitating her every move. Behind me, my little sister mirrored me. I held my baby brother close to my chest. We were a line of shadows, following our mother's sorrow through the house, our tiny hearts tethered to hers.

Eventually, we drifted back to bed, blanketed in silence and confusion. But I couldn't sleep. A nightmare jolted me awake. I left my bed, still half in a dream, and walked toward my mother's room. The hallway felt darker than usual. The air was thick, heavy. I had the sudden, chilling sensation I wasn't alone, that something unseen was behind me, getting closer. I broke into a run, heart thudding in my ears. When I crossed into her room, it felt like I ran into light. Not the glow of a lamp or TV but something softer. Something sacred. In the flickering light of the television, I saw a blur of a translucent presence. Peace washed over me. And then a voice, not outside me but inside, my voice but not mine, whispered: "*Everything will be alright.*" I collapsed onto her bed and was instantly asleep.

The next morning, I woke to the warmth of her kiss. Her face was tired. Her eyes looked far away. She was dressed in one of her suits. "Take care of my babies," she whispered. "I love you."

She turned and walked away. I watched her go. I didn't know it then but that would be the last time I'd watch my mother leave our home as a free woman.

A few hours later, the phone rang.

It was her. Her voice cracked with sorrow.

"Baby," she said, "Momma won't be coming home, okay?"

I didn't understand. "What do you mean?" I asked. "Are you just staying out a few more hours? Will you be back tonight?"

There was silence. Then, "I might be gone a couple of months... maybe a year."

I froze. My heart pounded. "But... how will we eat? Who's going to take care of us? Am I supposed to get a job now?"

She tried to reassure me. Said Grandma would be there soon. Told me to take care of my brother and sister. Told me she loved me. Told me to be strong.

But I was just a child with tears spilling down my face, a crying baby in my arms, and a confused little sister staring up at me for answers. That was the day I stopped being a kid and became something else: a stand-in mother, a keeper of secrets, a quiet warrior in the shadows.

Days later, my aunts came to clear out our apartment. My sister was taken to live across town. My baby brother and I were sent to a different relative. The three of us, once a unit, were torn apart like pages from a book.

I didn't tell anyone what had happened. Not my teachers. Not my friends. I wore my smile like armor. I hid my hurt like shame. The world wasn't built to understand girls like me.

I slipped into a kind of invisible grief. Depression. Fear. Silence. I floated through the years like a ghost, aching for answers, for connection, for someone, *anyone*, who could understand what I was carrying.

And then, during my freshman year of high school, I met her. Another girl. Same age. Same story. She was raising her little sister alone while her mother served time in prison. For the first time, I didn't feel like a secret. I felt seen.

I began to wonder: how many other children are living like this? Silently raising siblings, hiding the truth, carrying the shame of a parent's choices?

My mother was sentenced to sixteen years to life for refusing to testify against a violent man who threatened to kill her and her children. She chose silence to protect us. She served eight years before she was released for good behavior.

I still remember her first phone call home. She held a cell phone in her hand like it was a foreign object, laughing as she tried to figure it out. "You can talk on this thing?" she asked, in awe.

I had just finished a twelve-hour shift. When I got the call, my supervisor let me leave early. I drove four hours that day to see my mother, free for the first time in almost a decade. I'd dreamt of that day for years—of her spinning in the light, dressed in white.

That dream finally came true.

I kept every letter she wrote. I clung to every visit. I carried the sound of her voice in my bones. And when she came home, I finally found the words to tell our story.

Though this book is fictional, *Sixteen Years to Life* is inspired by real events: my life, our pain, our survival.

This story is for every child who knows what it feels like to lose a parent to the prison system. For every kid who has carried more than their share. For every secret kept. For every sleepless night. For every silent scream.

This book is for you.

Your beginning does not have to be your ending. You are not your pain. You are not alone.

Never stop dreaming of the light.

—Jamie Morrison

PART I

BEFORE THE FALL

The life I had before everything changed.

CHAPTER 1

The Good Life

My very first memory is of lying on an old, thick burgundy carpet, the kind that tickled your skin and smelled faintly of furniture polish and family dinners. Above me, the ceiling fan spun in slow, lazy circles, whispering through the silence like an old song. I'd watch those blades turn round and round, hypnotized, imagining they could lift me up and carry me somewhere magical, somewhere quiet and full of light.

My name is Jaydah. I was Momma's baby girl, skinny as a rail, light-skinned with wild, untamable hair. Momma called me her "doll baby," not just because of my size but because I came out of the womb tiny and delicate, something you'd place gently on a pillow and admire. Strangers used to stop us in the grocery store and coo over my little coils and bright eyes. "She's so precious," they'd say, and Momma would smile, but always kept one hand near my stroller. "She's cute but she bites," she'd warn. They didn't know—underneath the pretty face was a tiny terror. My nickname was Freddy Krueger. Get too close and I'd claw at your face with my baby nails like a wild cat.

I had a big brother named Dee, thirteen years old when I was four, tall and lean with a toffee complexion and a grin that always meant mischief. He was full of energy, always bouncing a ball, cracking a joke, or planning his next prank. Dee was the kind of brother who would sit on your head just to hear you scream, then laugh so hard he'd roll off like it was the funniest thing in the world. But as much as he loved to torment me, he loved me harder. Dee didn't just treat me like his sister. He treated me like I was his baby.

When we were younger, he'd pack me up in my pink dress, strap me into the stroller, and push me down the block to the basketball courts. I'd sit on the sidelines like the team mascot while he played with the neighborhood boys, always checking to make sure I was okay, tossing me a grin or a snack. When we got in trouble, which happened a lot, he'd volunteer, "Whup me first," he'd say, chest out. And she would. Dee would stand there, taking it like a champ, just to soften the blow for me and at times to pretend to act like me when I did get a whooping.

Our life felt full. Loud. Safe. We weren't rich, but Momma made sure we had what mattered: love, food, and a place to call home. She had deep brown skin, like polished mahogany, with a small waist and full hips that curved like a Coke bottle. Men noticed her. A lot of them. She was beautiful in that quiet, self-made way. Never flashy, but impossible to ignore. She worked hard, holding down jobs to take care of us, always tired but never too tired to kiss us goodnight. But for all her strength, I think Momma just wanted what most women want: love. Real love. The kind that protects you, stands beside you. The kind she kept looking for in all the wrong places.

Dee didn't live with us all the time. He floated between houses - grandma's, auntie's, cousins' - and I never really knew why. He didn't talk about it much but I could feel it in the way he tensed up around Momma's boyfriend.

Whenever he would leave, something shifted in our home. A light dimmed. A space opened up, and something dark crept in.

I would later have a name for it: Charles Walters.

Charles was tall, dark-skinned, and looked like he was mad at the world. His face was carved with rough edges, his eyes cold and empty like the inside of a locked room. He dressed like he had just stepped out of a prison yard with boots, creased dickies, and a stare that made your stomach twist. There was a heaviness that followed him into every room, like the air thickened when he walked through the door.

I didn't know then what kind of man he really was. But my spirit did. Even as a little girl, I felt it. The kind of fear that crawls under your skin and stays there.

That's how it began. The good life fading into something else, something harder, quieter, and difficult to escape.

CHAPTER 2

The Man in The Doorway

Dee always called me his baby doll. Not in that soft, mushy way either. He'd say it with his whole chest, with a crooked grin and swagger in his voice, tossing the words over his shoulder like a basketball pass. "Where my baby doll at?" he'd shout, voice bouncing off the walls as he swung open the front door, arms already stretched wide. And no matter where I was, I'd come running. Every single time.

Dee wasn't just my big brother. He was my safe place. My home inside the home. And as the house got darker, he was the only one who made it feel like light still lived there.

The more Charles came around, the more Dee did too. At first, I thought it was just a coincidence—Dee showing up with his jokes and his candy, playing one-on-one with me in the back alley, sneaking me honey buns and telling stories till I laughed so hard my belly hurt. But I noticed how he never left us alone if Momma wasn't home. He'd suddenly have a reason to stay longer. "Let me show you how to shoot a free throw, baby doll." "Let's walk to the corner store real quick." "You feel like going to the park for a bit?" Anything to keep us out of the apartment. Out of Charles' reach.

Charles wasn't a man, not really. He was more like a shadow that crept in and sucked the warmth out of every room he entered. Most people would call him a thug—tall and lean with skin like ash, eyes that didn't blink enough, and a greasy Jheri curl that left stains on every pillow, couch cushion, and shirt he leaned against. But to me, he was more like a slug. Slow. Grim. Impossible to get rid of. He smelled like stale beer and cigarettes and when he smiled—if you could call that stretch of skin a smile—my stomach twisted.

Something in my bones always tightened when he walked in, as if my spirit curled into a corner, hoping he wouldn't notice me. I'd shrink without meaning to, get quieter, smaller. I didn't know what fear was back then, not in a way I could name, but my body did. And so did Dee.

He knew something was off from the very beginning. He'd argue with Momma behind closed doors, voice rising and falling in muffled anger, but she'd wave him off like his concern was just another annoyance. "He's trying," she'd say. "He helps with the bills. He ain't perfect, but we need the help." But Dee wasn't fooled. Not for a second.

"If anything ever happens," he whispered to me once, kneeling in front of me, eyes serious, "you scream. You hear me, Baby Doll? Scream loud."

I nodded, because I always did what Dee said. I didn't fully understand why. But something in his voice made me believe I'd need to remember those words.

One night, everything changed.

The apartment was unusually quiet. Not peaceful—just still, like the air was holding its breath. Dee was sleeping in my room that night, crashed on a pallet beside my bed, one arm slung over his face, the other hanging off the mattress. I lay in bed, staring at the fan spinning above, its shadows cutting across the ceiling like slow-moving ghosts.

And then it happened.

The softest sound—the door creaking open just a hair—so light you might miss it. But not Dee. He stirred immediately. His eyes opened, sharp and alert. He didn't move. Just watched.

Charles stood in the doorway, backlit by the hallway light, his figure a solid block of darkness. He didn't speak. Didn't announce himself. Just slipped silently into the room like he'd done it before. Like it was nothing.

He walked slowly toward my bed and just stood there, staring down at me while I pretended to be asleep, my body frozen. Dee didn't make a sound. He told me later he didn't understand what he was seeing at first—just that something felt wrong. Off. Like watching a scene that wasn't meant for him.

After what felt like forever, Charles turned and walked out, the door clicking softly behind him.

The next morning, Dee didn't say much. He didn't joke. Didn't eat. Just sat there, quiet, staring at the table. When Momma came home, he pulled her aside. I couldn't hear everything, but I caught bits. "He was over her bed... watching her sleep... I saw him." Her voice cracked when she responded, like something inside her had snapped. "Dee... you know he wouldn't."

"Yes, he would."

Her face shifted between fear and denial, between wanting to protect her children and not knowing how to survive without him. She stood there, torn, and said nothing else.

Later that night, Dee packed his bag. Said he was going to stay with Grandma. For good this time. He kissed me on the forehead and said, "I'll still come visit, Baby Doll." And he did—but not like before. Not for long. Not enough. I could see the guilt in his eyes every time he looked at me, like he thought he was leaving me behind. But I didn't blame him. How could I? He was still just a boy himself. Trying to survive in a world that already asked too much of him.

And Charles stayed.

So did the silence.

I stopped running around the house. Stopped laughing so loud. I sat real still. I became smaller than I already was, trying to become invisible. One day, I stood in the living room while Charles sprawled on the couch, half-drunk, smelling like an old bar floor. I looked at his hairy legs, all knotted and ashy, and I pinched one of the wiry hairs with my little fingers.

"I oughta pull these out your ugly old legs," I said, puffing up the only courage I had left.

He looked down at me slowly, his eyes flat and cold. "If you did," he said, "I'd skin you alive."

I ran to Momma crying, repeating what he said, waiting for her to rage like she always did. But this time, she sighed and said, "Girl, you know he didn't mean that. Don't be so dramatic."

But I believed him.

It didn't take long before things got worse. Sometimes, when Momma was giving me a bath, he'd lean against the doorframe, arms crossed, smirking. Not saying a word. Just watching. His eyes lingered too long. His silence felt too loud. I didn't have the vocabulary for what that was, but I knew it was wrong. I could feel it in my chest, in my skin, in the way my stomach twisted itself in knots.

Then came the questions. The investigations. The dolls.

A woman in an office with soft hands and too much perfume asked me things I didn't understand. "Show me what happened using the dolls," she'd say, pushing them toward me. But I didn't want to play. I just wanted to go home.

Nightmares came like clockwork. Forests, fire, monsters with familiar faces. I'd wake up sweating, screaming, not sure where I was. Momma held me, rocked me, whispered that it was all just a dream. But it didn't feel like a dream. It felt like something I had lived through—something I couldn't unsee.

Eventually, Momma said I didn't have to go back to that office. Said I was too young to understand. Maybe she was right. But maybe that decision left pieces of me there, in that room, with that woman and those dolls.

It didn't matter. The damage had already taken root.

I started disappearing, inch by inch. Parts of me that used to laugh, to run, to dream—gone. I wasn't a little girl anymore. I was a watchful spirit in my own home. Quiet. Small. Careful.

So was my childhood.

It slipped away the day Charles came and it never really came back.

CHAPTER 3

The Big House

After Charles was finally gone, life began to feel lighter again. Not perfect—just lighter. The tension in the air lifted and for the first time in a long time, Momma exhaled. The way she moved through the house changed. She played music again. She laughed more. Even her hugs felt fuller, less distracted. And Dee started coming around more too, cracking jokes, hiding behind corners to scare us, bringing back the laughter that had been absent for too long.

That's when Momma decided it was time to go home.

Truly home.

We called it the Big House.

Not because of its size (it wasn't grand by any means) but because of its heart. The Big House was the place Granddaddy built with his bare hands, brick by brick, after saving every cent he could from working sunup to sundown. He was a quiet man but every time the jar of coins on the kitchen counter filled, he smiled a little wider, knowing he was one step closer to building a future for his family. That house wasn't just wood and brick. It was a symbol. A monument of protection. A love letter sealed in foundation.

After Grandma moved into a smaller apartment across town, Aunt Rita inherited the house. But no one ever really owned it. It belonged to all of us. That house was the kind of place you could return to after the world knocked you down. It didn't matter if you lost your job, your partner, your way—those front steps were a reset button. The threshold held healing.

Momma and Aunt Rita were the youngest of nine kids, just two years apart. Grandma always said her gray hairs were earned raising seven girls and that the last two almost took her out. But no girls were closer than Momma and Rita. They were more than sisters. They were a tag team, a two-woman army. They shared chores, laughter, grudges, and now, parenting.

I was six months older than Chad and two years older than Carmen. The three of us were raised like siblings instead of cousins. We ate from the same plate, fought for the same toy, matched from head to toe in outfits our mothers picked out. We were a little tribe—laughing, bickering, making up in the same breath.

Carmen and I had so many identical outfits that even now, we could open each other's closets and find clothes we both remembered from childhood. Our moms dressed us like twins. And I didn't mind. She was my cousin, my best friend, my shadow. We were inseparable, running in the backyard, watching cartoons side by side, falling asleep mid-conversation under one blanket. We fussed, but we loved harder.

The house itself buzzed with energy. Rita worked days while Momma worked nights. One would be frying pork chops, the other doing heads in the living room. They passed each other like ships, tagging in and out of motherhood, household chores, and discipline. It worked. It worked beautifully. The bills stayed paid. Bellies stayed full. And there was always a song playing low in the background or a stern "Cut that mess out!" echoing from a hallway.

Honestly, those days were the happiest I can remember from my childhood.

I remember one afternoon like a scene from a movie. Momma was laid across the bed, tangled in the long, curly phone cord, giggling with someone on the line. Rita was at work, so Momma was the sheriff on duty. Carmen, Chad, and I were upstairs where we were supposed to be quiet and behaving. But, of course, we weren't.

Momma had a clear plastic box filled with watches she bought wholesale to resell for extra money. Fancy ones, gold-plated, leather-banded, shiny things that sparkled in the light. To us, they were treasure. To me, they were science projects.

We cracked them open with screwdrivers and scissors, dissecting each tiny gear like budding engineers. Guts of watches spilled across the carpet. We were mid-surgery when Momma walked in.

Her voice froze the air. "Oh my God."

The box lay open like a treasure chest pillaged by pirates.

Tiny springs and wheels were everywhere.

She didn't yell. She didn't even move. She just stood there, belt in hand, like a silent executioner.

Then came the words: "You can't go outside until you get your whooping."

Outside was freedom. No jump rope. No bikes. No hot pavement games unless we faced justice.

"She your momma," Chad said, shrugging at me.

He was right.

I stepped out of hiding first. My legs shook, but I stood tall. I peeked around the door, trying out my softest voice. "Momma... we didn't mean to. We were just trying to fix them."

She didn't say anything at first. Then she smiled and said, "Come give Momma a kiss."

I took the bait. Skipped over like all was forgiven. And the moment my lips touched her cheek—WHAP! Over her knee I went. She gave me three clean pops and stood me back up like nothing happened. "Go get the others," she said, wiping my tears with the same hands that held the belt.

Carmen had buried herself under the bed, gripping the floor like her life depended on it. I laid on my belly and whispered, "It wasn't that bad. You can do it."

"No," she whimpered, her voice shaking. "It's gonna hurt."

Eventually, Momma called out in her gentlest voice. "Carmen, come on, baby. If you come out now, I won't whoop you."

Lie. Trap.

Carmen emerged slow, cautious, halfway through when Momma snatched her shirt and gave her the same three pops. Carmen screamed like her world ended, but when it was over, Momma pulled her close and kissed her forehead.

"Y'all can go outside now. Love you."

It was strange—getting punished and affirmed in the same moment. But that was Momma. She believed in tough love. "I whoop you because I love you," she'd say. "It hurts me more than it hurts you."

And I'd think, "then why you swing that belt like it's personal?"

But I never said it. I just wiped my face and ran outside, sun hitting my cheeks like grace.

Those days at the Big House were golden. The world outside had its storms, but that house was our calm. We had food, warmth, laughter, and each other. We slept soundly, wrapped in the arms of people who showed up for us every single day.

It was the last time I remember feeling completely like a child.

Not long after that, everything changed again.

CHAPTER 4

New Sister, New World

Of course I was spoiled rotten. I'd been Momma's little baby for a few years now, the center of her world. Her shadow. Her heartbeat. We did everything together—ate together, napped together, even danced barefoot on the linoleum floor to Anita Baker playing through the little clock radio she kept by the stove. She'd sing along, curling my hair in her lap, laughing when I tried to hit the high notes. We were two peas in a pod. And I held onto that love like it was mine alone because for a while, it was.

But that season didn't last long.

I was six years old the day my whole world shifted. I stood on tiptoes over the edge of a hospital bassinet and locked eyes with a chubby-faced, chocolate-colored baby whose lashes curled toward the heavens and whose thick, coiled hair already outshined mine. Her name was Bianca.

My new little sister.

At first, I was curious. I poked gently at her blanket. Watched her mouth wiggle when she yawned. But curiosity turned quickly to something else. Resentment. Envy. She was a stranger who had just stolen the only thing in this world I'd ever had all to myself—Momma's love. And just like that, I wasn't the baby anymore.

From that moment on, life changed.

Everything I had, I had to split in two. Candy bars. Attention. Even my little pink room with the rainbows on the walls. "She's your little sister," Momma would say, placing Bianca's toys next to mine, putting our names together like a set: "Jaydah and Bianca." It didn't matter I'd had friends first or that my bed came with my name carved in stickers on the headboard. Everything became shared. Even love.

And I knew I had a role now. I was the big sister.

Shortly after Bianca was born, Momma moved us again, this time to a better side of town. The apartment was a little bigger, the neighborhood a little cleaner. She was always chasing a better life, trying to keep us ahead of whatever storm was chasing behind her. We left behind some of the cousins I was closest to—Chad and Carmen mostly—but visited Granny's on weekends. It wasn't the same. Everything felt quieter. A little colder.

Momma worked hard to make sure we were good. She made it her mission to keep food in the fridge, clothes washed and folded, hair greased and parted just right for school. She did it all, even when she had nothing left to give. I watched her disappear into long hours, working security or double shifts, just to keep the lights on.

When she was gone, I took care of Bianca.

At just six years old, I had a routine. I'd wake myself up early, brush my teeth, and do my best to get Bianca ready for the day. Her hair was a full-time job by itself. I'd tug and braid and try to smooth it down with water and grease, only to have it frizz right back up. Then I'd fight her into a clean outfit, pack her little bag for daycare, grab the check Momma left on the counter, and push the stroller to drop her off. Some days I'd get lucky and make it to school on time. Other days I'd be late or end up walking the whole way because I missed the bus again. But I did it. Because that's what big sisters do.

I didn't know that most kids didn't have to do what I did.

Didn't know that at six, I was living like I was sixteen.

There was one morning I'll never forget. I had missed the bus—again—and decided to walk. I was halfway down the street when a white pickup truck slowed beside me. A middle-aged white man leaned out the window.

"You headed to school?" he asked.

My whole body went stiff. My heart pounded so loud it drowned out the sound of his engine. All I could hear was Momma's voice in my head warning me about strangers, especially men, especially white men. I didn't know what he wanted, but I knew what could happen. I nodded anyway.

The ride was quiet. Every few seconds, I felt his eyes flick up toward the rearview mirror, watching me. I kept my gaze locked on the road, praying he'd just keep driving. When we finally pulled up to the school, I didn't wait. I swung the door open before the truck stopped and took off running toward the front entrance.

That night, I dreamed I was being chased through a forest. A man with devil horns and fire-red eyes was behind me, grabbing at the hem of my dress. Blood poured from the sky like rain. I woke up drenched in sweat, screaming for Momma. I didn't tell her about the man in the truck. I just crawled into her bed and laid beside her, holding my breath so I could hear her heartbeat.

Sometimes I thought maybe if Momma had a good man, one who stayed and protected us, we wouldn't have to worry so much. I started imagining who that could be. Keisha's daddy seemed like a good choice. He was kind, had a steady job, and raised Keisha all by himself. I made it my mission to hook them up. Even Keisha was on board. But when we brought it up to Momma, she just shook her head. "I'm not dating nobody right now."

So I made Keisha's house my second home. After dropping off Bianca at daycare, I'd rush over and eat breakfast with them, pretend I was part of their family. It felt safe there. It felt normal.

Back home, Momma had picked up a job working security at Dell. It paid the bills but pulled her away even more. I could see it wearing on her—and on me. She could too. She quit and went back to her roots, doing hair. It was in her blood. It gave her freedom. And it gave us more time together. She found a shop near Granny and moved us to Dallas. That was the beginning of something better.

For the first time in a long time, I got to be a kid again.

There was laughter in the house. Holidays with real food, cousins running through Granny's backyard, music playing in the kitchen. Bianca had people to play with. I had time to just breathe.

I was still the protector. Still Momma's little soldier. But now, I wasn't doing it alone.

CHAPTER 5

Steel Toe Truth

By the time I was ten, Bianca was four and full of light. Her skin had deepened into the color of warm chocolate, her cheeks soft and doll-like. Her laugh could slice through the thickest tension and sometimes I wondered if she even noticed the chaos swirling around us. Maybe she did. Maybe her sweetness was just her armor.

Dee had joined the Navy, Momma had started working at a local beauty shop, and we lived in a two-bedroom apartment with peeling white walls, our two pet hamsters, and, unfortunately, the new boyfriend.

Reggie came with the apartment like a roach you didn't see during the tour. He first showed up when Momma was moving us in, flashing that smooth smile like he was doing her a favor. Next thing I knew, he never left. No job. No schedule. Just charm, presence, and a growing collection of shady visitors.

At first, I liked him. I mean, what 10-year-old questions the source of new toys and full cabinets? Reggie made sure we didn't want for much—at least in the beginning. Momma was glowing for a while. She'd hum while she cooked, sway while she cleaned.

Reggie called her "Queen," bought her things, and gave Bianca dollar bills to stay quiet when he was "handling business."

But even back then, I wasn't stupid. A grown man sleeping all day and up all night, with folks showing up carrying TVs, baby clothes, and bags that rattled too much or too little—that's not a nine-to-five. That's a hustle. I started to see the cracks even before Momma did.

The biggest crack? Her bedroom door. Locked. All the time.

Momma had never locked us out before. Before Reggie, Bianca and I used to climb into bed with her at night—one of us in the bend of her knee, the other at her side. That bed was our safe place. Warm, full of laughter and lotion-scented hugs. But now, her room had become something different. Something closed. Something dark.

I stopped asking to come in. Eventually, I stopped wondering what was on the other side.

What didn't stop were the fights.

At first, they came once every few weeks—loud yelling, slamming doors. Eventually, it felt like every other night. I'd lie in my bed and listen. At ten years old, I had already mastered the art of measuring violence: the difference between arguing and breaking. I knew that as long as it was yelling, I could stay in bed. But if something crashed, if Momma screamed a certain kind of scream, I'd bolt out of bed.

Bianca would usually be sitting in the hallway, thumb in her mouth, wide-eyed, watching. That was my cue. I'd charge in, screaming at Reggie, grabbing whatever part of him I could reach—shirt, wrist, belt. Kicking and clawing. I don't think he ever wanted us to see him like that, because once we stepped into the room, the beatings usually stopped.

But the damage was already done.

That year, I started calling 911. I didn't do it every time, but I knew how. Momma would tell me after the fact how she'd thrown out all his clothes and electronics, how she stood up to him, how she wasn't afraid. But I had seen the look in her eyes after those nights—eyes that were tired, swollen, and full of something I didn't recognize in her: defeat.

Still, I believed her. I wanted to believe she was strong enough to fight back. That she had it under control. I needed to believe it. Because if she couldn't win, then what hope was there for me and Bianca?

But that belief shattered the night of the steel toe.

It started with a crash. Something heavy and loud—glass, maybe. Then more yelling, louder this time. I opened my door just in time to see Momma stumbling backward and a steel toe boot flying at her stomach. It hit. Hard. She crumpled like a paper doll.

I couldn't breathe. The hallway felt like it was closing in around me, and my vision tunneled until all I could see was her. Spit foamed at the corners of her mouth, and she crawled toward the kitchen, one hand clutching her side. The woman who had once danced with me in the living room, who told me I was her strong girl, was now gagging on the floor.

Then Bianca screamed.

I turned to see her at our door, frozen. Her face—God, I'll never forget it. That was the first time she saw what I had been shielding her from. The magic of childhood ripped away in one moment.

I ran to her, pulled her into the room, told her it was just a game. "Momma, Reggie, and me—we're playing," I lied. And for the first time, she believed me. She sat quietly, hugging her stuffed bear while I stepped back into the hell.

I grabbed our Mickey Mouse phone and dialed 911.

"911, what's your emergency?"

"My mom—my mom needs help. Her boyfriend is hurting her—"

"Put the phone down!" Momma screamed. "Jaydah, please! I'm okay!"

But I wasn't. None of us were.

The door burst open. Reggie stood there, breathing hard. His silhouette blocked all the light, and his eyes had no soul in them. He reached out and snatched the phone from my hand, slamming it back onto the receiver. He didn't say a word. Just turned around and left.

The front door slammed. Silence fell.

I found Momma on the floor, wiping her face. She smiled like nothing happened, said she made herself throw up because she was so mad. She even joked about not messing up the carpet.

I wanted to scream at her. Tell her that none of this was normal. That love didn't feel like this. But I didn't. I just helped her to the couch, brought her water, and sat next to her while she breathed shallow and slow.

Later that night, she told me about the gun.

"I was on my knees, Jaydah. He pulled the trigger. Right at my head." She whispered it like a prayer. "It clicked, but nothing came out. Just air. That was God."

I nodded, but all I could think was: What if next time it wasn't?

I didn't sleep that night. I lay in my bed, watching Bianca's chest rise and fall. I thought about how I could protect her. What would happen if Momma didn't survive the next fight? If Reggie came for us?

Hate bloomed quietly in my chest. Thick and heavy.

I wasn't afraid of Reggie anymore. I just hated him. I hated what he did to Momma, to our home, to the softness we used to have. I hated the way he laughed when he thought no one was watching. I hated his lies, his breath, his face. I hated how I still couldn't do anything.

That hate matured me.

The next time he came back, I watched him differently. He brought toys. Money. Stuff to smooth things over. But my eyes didn't soften. I took his gifts, sure. But I promised myself I'd never forget. I kept every memory like a sharp stone in my pocket, waiting for the right time to throw them all back at him.

The steel toe truth was this: love doesn't hit, love doesn't scream, love doesn't lock you out and tell you it's for your safety.

But at ten years old, I had to hold all of that in my heart without it breaking.

CHAPTER 6

The Weight of Being Eleven

The new apartment felt like a dream compared to the chaos we'd come from. It was a two-story townhome with three full bedrooms, and our balcony overlooked a large pool and a steaming hot tub that always looked better than it probably was. From up there, it looked like we had finally moved into something better—more peaceful, more secure.

But peace is not a place. It's not square footage or a view.

Peace didn't live with us.

The fights between Reggie and Momma hadn't stopped. They just grew quieter, more calculated. I had gotten so used to the yelling that I knew the rhythm of their arguments—when the tension would rise, when the slamming would start, and when I needed to intervene. When the voices stayed raised but the hands stayed still, I'd listen from bed, frozen. But the moment I heard something crash or Momma's voice break differently, I would be in that room in seconds—yelling, screaming, kicking at Reggie until he backed off. He never really hit her when he knew we were watching. I think somewhere deep down, even he knew some things couldn't be unseen.

I was only eleven years old.

And I was tired.

Tired in my spirit, like I had lived decades longer than the days on the calendar. I found myself shifting between moments of laughter and tears with no warning. One second I'd be joking with Bianca, and the next I'd be sobbing in the bathroom for reasons I couldn't explain. I didn't have the language to name depression, but I felt the heaviness of it resting on my chest like a stack of bricks. I didn't feel like a child. I felt like the backbone of a crumbling world.

Sometimes I'd watch those sad movies or public service ads on TV—stories about teenagers who swallowed too many pills and didn't wake up. Part of me wondered if they felt like I did. Trapped. Small. Like their lives had been signed away before they ever got to make a choice.

One day, I pretended to be sick just to stay home. Bianca left for school and I sat on the bed in silence, peeling the wrapper off a honey bun I'd hidden under the mattress just for days like this. I chewed slowly, letting my mind wander. Where was my daddy? Why hadn't he sent a card in all these years? I remembered he was so light-skinned he could pass for white. Maybe he looked at me, at my dark brown skin, and decided I couldn't be his daughter.

That thought stung deeper than I let on.

Momma stayed with Reggie even though he brought more hurt than healing. I knew it wasn't just about love. He provided—maybe not peace or safety—but material things. Groceries. Rent. Presents for Bianca and me when he wanted to make himself look good. That was enough for her to stay.

Maybe I was a mistake. Maybe I wasn't supposed to be here.

I walked to the bathroom and opened the cabinet. There was a bottle of ibuprofen in the back. I didn't know what it was exactly, but I knew it dulled pain. I grabbed a glass of water from the kitchen and sat back down on the edge of my bed, tears rolling down my cheeks. I placed the pills on my tongue, one by one, and swallowed.

I don't remember how many I took. Just enough to think it would end the ache in my heart.

I lay down and waited. The room started spinning slowly, my body feeling heavy and loose like a balloon drifting out of a child's hand. I don't know when I fell asleep.

When I woke up, I was still here.

The first thing I thought was: You can't even do this right.

Then I heard Momma's keys jingling at the front door.

Panic hit me like a wave. I scrambled to hide the pill bottle, poured out the rest of the water, and ran into the living room with the fakest smile I could manage.

"Hey, baby," Momma said, kissing the top of my head.

"You feelin' better?"

I nodded, not trusting my voice. There was a lump in my throat that threatened to burst.

She looked down at me with the kind of love that makes your heart break. The kind that lets you know that no matter how flawed your world is, someone still sees you as worthy of everything. I knew right then that if she had come home and found me lifeless in that bed, it would've destroyed her. That was the last time I ever tried anything like that. I didn't want to be the reason my momma's light went out.

Later that week, Reggie brought over two of his daughters – Latoya and Tonya. Their mother, I later found out, was in prison too. Of course, it was because of him. He had a trail of women and children left in the mess he made, none of whom he stayed with for long.

I never called him Daddy. To me, he was just another grown boy pretending to be a man.

But Latoya and Tonya weren't the problem. We all got along just fine. We were four little Black girls who understood too much too early—who had learned to babysit siblings, heat up leftovers, and keep secrets. There was no judgment between us. Just silent understanding.

Still, I needed to escape. I built a life in my imagination through TV shows where families ate dinner together and dads tucked their daughters in. I stayed outside as long as I could, playing with kids from the complex, pretending that I was just like them. I'd laugh louder, talk more, and carry myself like someone who had nothing to hide.

But once those streetlights flickered on, I ran home fast. Not because I was afraid of the dark, but because I knew coming home late meant trouble.

That summer, I met a girl named Nia. Her apartment was just a few buildings down, and she became my getaway. I begged Momma to let me stay the night at her place, but the answer was always no. She didn't trust nobody, not after everything she'd seen. But eventually, she caved. On one condition: Bianca had to come too.

I rolled my eyes and fussed, but secretly, I didn't mind. Bianca was my shadow. She followed me everywhere, and most days I liked it.

Nia's apartment felt different—like fresh air. Her mom let us be wild, loud, and free. When we got there, I noticed right away her mom had gone to work, leaving us alone with her older brother. He was maybe a year or so older than us but he moved like he had something to prove.

He walked around shirtless, flexing muscles he didn't really have, trying to show off. It made me uncomfortable, but I kept quiet, pretending I didn't care.

Later that night, he wanted to play a game.

"What kind of game?" I asked.

He just smirked. Nia looked at me and said softly, "It'll hurt a little, but it's okay."

My stomach twisted. Something didn't feel right. But I stayed silent.

The lights went out. He told us to hide.

But I wasn't hiding. I was on guard.

When he found me, he pinned me down, tried to kiss me, touched places I didn't want him to touch. Nia whispered that it would be okay, but I didn't listen. I fought him off with everything in me.

I made it through the night with my body still mine.

I walked home early the next morning, my head held high. When I told Momma what happened, she was furious. She called Nia's mom and cursed her out for leaving us with that boy. When she hung up, she pulled me close and said, "I'm proud of you for speaking up. For knowing what to do."

That night, I lay on my bed staring at the ceiling fan, the blades spinning in slow circles like the thoughts in my head. I was only eleven, but I felt forty. I had fought off a boy, buried a suicide attempt, and protected my sister from shadows no child should face.

I was growing up, but not in the way little girls should.

And still—I was here.

Still fighting.

Still surviving.

Still learning what it meant to carry the weight of being eleven.

PART II

AFTER THE SENTENCE

Shattered with one fall of the gavel.

CHAPTER 7
Broken Hinge

For a little while, things almost seemed normal. Not quiet —but calm enough to give the illusion of peace. Reggie wasn't disappearing for days anymore, and the stream of strangers at our doorstep slowed to a trickle. The usual parade of homeless folks looking for a place to lay their heads had become fewer. But in their place came a different kind of visitor: women. Not just any women— women whose eyes were heavy and who smelled like late nights and bad choices.

I learned how to recognize them quickly. Lip gloss too shiny, eyeliner smudged like it had been slept in, and a hollow kind of laughter that came out loud but meant nothing. They weren't there to visit Momma or check in on us kids. They came with Reggie. They followed him around like smoke trails, clinging to him in ways I couldn't understand.

I kept quiet, mostly because I had learned when to listen more than I spoke. But inside, I was watching everything. I watched Momma act like she didn't see the way Reggie leaned in close when he whispered in one woman's ear. I watched her grip her cup tighter at the kitchen table when he went missing for hours only to reappear with cologne on his collar and no explanations. Still, she let it slide.

"Keep an eye on my cup, baby," she'd say to me every time company came over. It had become a ritual, a task she passed to me without ever needing to explain why. I knew the streets she came from. I knew what could happen to a woman if she left her drink unguarded. So I stayed close. I stayed sharp.

Reggie treated Bianca and me surprisingly well, like we were ornaments of his good side. He brought candy, handed us cash to run down to the store, told jokes that only sometimes landed. But none of that meant I trusted him. I understood something about his world, saw the look in his eyes when things didn't go his way. I knew what it meant when the air got still around him.

And I knew—peace wouldn't last.

One Saturday morning, I woke up to Bianca sitting quietly on her bed, holding a folded bill in her hand.

"Reggie gave me this and told me to stay in here and be quiet," she whispered.

That was all I needed to hear. I threw on a pair of sweatpants and a T-shirt and headed downstairs, alert and already irritated. If Momma had been home, none of this would be happening. She didn't allow certain kinds of people in her house—not unless she was there to supervise. That day, though, she wasn't.

The living room was thick with smoke and laughter. A few of Reggie's regulars were spread across the worn furniture —hoarse laughter spilling out, beer cans clinking, cards slapping the table. Reggie leaned back in the recliner, toothpick in his mouth, arms slung over the back like he owned the place. He barely glanced at me.

"Where's Momma?" I asked, standing in the hallway.

"Out," he replied, like that one word was enough to dismiss me.

I didn't like the energy in the room. The way one man's eyes followed me when I walked to the kitchen. The way the women giggled but it sounded more like desperation than joy. I busied myself with wiping counters and keeping Bianca in the room. I didn't want her anywhere near the front of the house. If something went down, I needed to make sure she stayed safe.

As the sun dipped behind the horizon, the guests trickled out in twos and threes. Reggie disappeared sometime after nine, slipping out the front door without a word. I stood by the window, waiting. Momma still wasn't home.

I couldn't sleep.

I kept pacing the floor, glancing at the clock, hoping to hear the jingle of her keys at the door. But hours passed, and nothing. At some point, I must've fallen asleep, too exhausted to keep watch.

The sound of her voice the next morning startled me awake. I sat up straight, blinking the sleep out of my eyes, my heart racing.

"Momma?" I called out, my voice cracking.

"In here, baby."

She was in the kitchen, pulling her hair up into a bun like nothing had happened. Bianca was sitting on the counter eating dry cereal straight from the box, kicking her legs and talking to herself. I walked in slowly, trying to read the room. Momma turned around, smiling, like she had just gotten back from church.

"Where were you?" I asked.

"I needed a break," she said, stretching. "Got myself a hotel room. Took a hot bath. Ordered food I didn't have to cook. Watched movies till I fell asleep."

"You didn't call," I said, sharper than I meant to.

"I wanted to, but they didn't allow calls from the rooms," she replied, not missing a beat.

I didn't believe her. But I didn't say that. I knew better than to challenge her directly. Instead, I followed her into the living room as she moved about the apartment like everything was fine.

Then I saw it.

The bathroom door was busted—the hinge torn straight off from top to bottom, and the lock dangled uselessly. I froze. My stomach twisted. That kind of damage didn't come from an accident. I didn't say anything, just kept walking. But as I moved through the kitchen, I noticed the broken glass on the counter, a cabinet door hanging open like it had been ripped.

Something had happened. And she was lying to cover it up.

Back in the kitchen, Momma was putting eggs in the pan like we were about to have the perfect Sunday morning. I waited a minute, then quietly asked, "What really happened?"

She paused, spatula in hand. "Girl, I told you. Reggie got mad because I left without telling him. I came back and we argued. I got mad and started throwing things."

"Did you bust down the bathroom door?" I asked.

She turned and looked at me, eyes narrowing. "He locked himself in there. I wasn't about to let him hide."

But I knew the truth. I knew she was the one who had locked herself in, probably trying to get away from him. I knew it was his hands that shattered that glass, his voice that filled the room with rage, not hers. And I hated him for it.

The next day, he showed up like nothing had happened. He had toys in his hands, a bottle of perfume in a gift bag, and that slick smile that made my skin crawl.

I watched him from the hallway. He placed the gifts down on the table and acted like he was Santa Claus. Bianca squealed, hugging the teddy bear. Momma thanked him quietly, the muscles in her face tight.

He looked at me and extended a small box—earrings, probably. I took it, nodded, and as soon as he turned his back, I rolled my eyes so hard they nearly got stuck.

He didn't fool me. I knew what he was.

And I knew one day, I was going to make him regret every time he made my mother feel like she had to lie to her own daughter.

I wasn't a little girl anymore. I was watching. I was learning. And if he ever put his hands on her again, I would be ready.

CHAPTER 8

Unfaithful

It was a breezy, sunlit afternoon—the perfect sort of day you'd imagine yourself lying in tall grass, staring at drifting clouds, daydreaming of all the things you wanted to become. I felt light, like that girl, floating on possibilities. But as I stepped onto the landing of our second-floor apartment, a storm crashed through the open front door: shouting, thundering footsteps, a crash of electronics and clothes hurled over the balcony railing.

"Damn," I thought. "What is it now?"

My heart pounded. I climbed the narrow stairs two at a time, adrenaline fueling every step. At the top, I saw Momma straining to shove our big-screen TV toward the door. Her face was set, her brow deep in stripped furrows I'd never seen before.

"What's going on, Mom? What happened?" I called.

Silence, except low, trembling cursing that rattled her lips. Through the chaos of the hallway, I caught Reggie's voice echoing inside the apartment:

"You crazy bitch, don't you fuck up my T.V. I'm about to whoop yo ass!"

Then another woman's taunt, rising above his:

"Yeah, bitch! Right here on yo' couch!"

Heat rose in me. Momma dropped the TV, whirled at full force down the hallway, and I followed in her wake, heart hammering like a war drum. She reached the other woman first, swinging until her arms shook, landing heavy blows.

I stood frozen, thinking she moved like lightning—how even caught off guard, she found power, fury. *Yes, Momma!*

Reggie stepped between them, arm outstretched. I saw the shock on Momma's face—but she still slapped him so hard his head snapped back. His eyes went wide, wild, like he'd seen God Himself.

I couldn't wait. I stormed in, lungs burning, fists clenched.

"If you even *touch* my momma—" I spat, choking for breath. "I know what you do, I know your life—if you lay a finger on her, it's on *you*, too!"

Silence crashed in response.

He glared at me, straight-eyed, step by step like a predator. I stayed in his path, chin raised, voice steady.

He moved toward Momma. She tried to back away—but one misstep, and she stumbled, tripping down the last three stairs. Reggie paused, then closed in—but didn't touch her. I heard sirens through my ears. His cowardice gave me hope—he wouldn't risk a police stop in front of witnesses.

The other woman screeched, but I didn't listen. I lunged past her and stomped on a chunk of her weave lying on the balcony floor. Satisfaction. Momma didn't need me, but I felt her need me.

Next, I saw the box—Reggie's secret stash, his money, dope—his empire. I grabbed it, wrenched it from his hands, and threw it over the balcony. Rocks and bills rattled as they hit the concrete below. He froze, stunned, then scrambled after it, snatching up the bits before anyone else saw.

His female partner, mouth open like an insulted bird, glared at me. I stared back. No fear. No respect.

Reggie raced back toward the apartment. My heart pounded. He came so close I could smell his breath. He opened his mouth to scream, but I slapped it shut, body tense:

"Bitch, touch me, and I'll *make sure* you never see the light of day. Kiss your fifty million fucking kids goodbye—this is a promise."

His face clenched. No finger raised. He turned, grabbed the woman's arm and marched out.

Momma limped toward me. Sweat glistened on her brow. Her ankle was swollen and she began to gag, clutching at the stairs. She vomited on her shirt.

"Good," she said through clenched teeth. "I didn't get it on the carpet."

My mind screamed—*Momma, your ankle!*

I grabbed the phone, dialed 911 with trembling fingers.

Paramedics came fast. Momma wiped off, changed clothes. She told me to get Bianca. "Call Granny," she said. Her voice shook. I felt the ground drop away. During the summer, our place would have been full of Reggie's hangers-on—but after that, everyone cleared out. That summer dragged on. No one returned. And I came close— *so close*—to losing my mom, losing what had kept me moving through all of that.

Over the next few days, the apartment air felt still and sharp. Momma had to work to afford her swelling ankle treatment, and I took on extra chores—washing, cooking, cleaning, keeping Bianca out of trouble, making sure nobody saw our bruises.

The tension in the apartment, when there was no shouting, was worse than the fights. Every creak of the door, every step in the hall made me flinch. Something had cracked in us.

Momma's ankle slowly healed, though it remained swollen for weeks. Granny came by more. She looked at us, looked at Momma's bruised cheek and swollen ankle, the tears in my eyes, and said nothing at first. She just hugged us hard and packed us in her car to stay at her house.

She told Momma: "If he comes back around, you call me—day or night. He ain't worth no fuckin' trouble."

Momma closed her eyes, nodded.

We had no family summer vacations that year. No trips to

the park. No playing in sprinklers. Instead, I watched Momma stare out windows, wait at the door, check the hallway. I cooked all the meals we could afford, refused to wear Momma's old heels even once, knowing how much she sacrificed.

I developed a new rhythm: wake, feed Bianca, pack lunches, drop her at daycare, work my after-school babysitting shift, come home, scrub, mend clothes, help Momma wrap the ankle, read to her, pray before bedtime that Reggie stayed gone. And every night, I dreamt of him returning.

But he didn't. He stayed away.

Then came the Sunday when Momma knocked a plate off the balcony, sending it crashing into dust below, stunned me again.

She had old cracks under her forehead—hard lines born of stress. That morning, she was throwing dishes off the porch like she was erasing evidence—clocks, plates, clothes—and I caught her dragging the last load toward a white panel van in the driveway. I asked what happened.

Momma's voice shook: "He outside demanding I give him money, told me he wasn't sorry. I told him he needed to get help, and he snapped. He said I was trash... you know what he called me."

She spat the words like venom. Then she grabbed the TV remote and threw it, cracking his car's windshield.

I stood stunned. She retreated and collapsed on the porch, my arms around her. She cried. I helped her inside.

Reggie showed up again two nights later: thumping music, bright headlights in the parking lot, loud voices. I rushed to the window to see him tearing through momma's belongings—wallet, papers, shoes—throwing them down the walkway. He'd made his way inside the apartment just to terrorize her.

I grabbed Bianca and locked us inside the bedroom. We didn't sleep until we knew Momma was inside her room, he was gone, and all the doors were locked.

Some mornings, Momma would stand at the mirror, carefully combing tangled hair, applying makeup. I'd help her dress—pinstripes or khakis, depending on her meeting.

"Momma, you okay?"

She'd look at me and the creases under her eyes would smooth for a moment. She'd smile, straightening her shoulders: "One day at a time, baby."

I felt proud. Something fierce and protective was growing in me.

That fall, the afternoon sun warmed our living room. I sat on the floor, coloring, when I heard the click of keys in the lock. Momma stepped inside—quiet, careful. She closed the door.

She dropped her purse, pulled me close and said:

"You did good today. Granny told me you're learning fast." I hugged her, breathing in her scent—jasmine and hope.

The days stretched on. I made sure the house held warmth. I cooked rice and beans, watered the sad geranium by the window, asked Momma to show me how to iron.

She taught me to fold shirts into crisp rectangles, to tuck sheets with hospital corners, to thread needles for sewing.

"You'll learn," she said, "and you'll stay ready. Cause I ain't staying down for no man."

I realized something: I'd become the anchor. Not Reggie. Not any of the men we had known. Not even Momma herself.

In the mirror, I saw Momma's reflection more often than my own—her head tilt, her quiet shoulders. I smiled until my cheeks hurt.

I began wearing her old bracelets when I went to school, tiny gold hoops, snapped open to hang from my ears. They reminded me of her. Of strength.

And though tears still pricked heavy at night, I slept good. I knew we were moving forward—even if slowly. There would be scars in the carpet but not in us, not anymore.

Momma held me close and whispered:

"Baby girl, always stand. Don't let nobody do you wrong.

Not a man, nor a boy—no one."

I nodded, closed my eyes.

I was growing up. Bending but never broken.

CHAPTER 9

Unwanted Attention

That Christmas break was the most memorable one I ever had—and not in the ways a kid would hope. There were no snowball fights, no holiday cheer that made me feel warm inside. Just a growing awareness that something about me had changed. I couldn't name it then, but I could feel it in the way the world started looking at me. I didn't look like a child much anymore.

My body was growing faster than I could understand it.

Breasts. Hips. Curves I hadn't asked for. I was still the same scrappy, bare-faced girl on the inside, the one who liked to catch fireflies and walk barefoot through puddles, but suddenly people treated me like I was someone else. Someone older. Someone available.

Boys started staring too long. Men started whispering. Their eyes felt like they stripped away parts of me I wasn't ready to lose. And the worst part? I couldn't tell if it was in my head or if I was really being seen like that. But deep down, I knew.

It all started the week before Christmas. Momma woke me up early, kissed my forehead, and handed me the Lone Star food stamp card along with a list longer than I expected. "Just a few things," she'd said. I rolled my eyes and pulled the covers off.

"Few" was never just a few.

I got dressed, tugging on a hoodie that no longer quite fit the way it used to. I noticed how tight my jeans had become, how the hoodie didn't fall as long as it used to. I wrapped a jacket around my waist, hoping it would help hide what I couldn't.

The store was only across the street, but I hated the walk. It wasn't the walk itself—it was the stares, the cars that slowed down just a little too much, the feeling something could happen, someone could say or do something that would ruin my whole day.

I paced the aisles, moving fast but not too fast. I didn't want to draw attention. I had developed this quiet ritual: scan the crowd, choose the shortest line, avoid eye contact. I'd clutch the card tight in my hand and prepare myself for the moment the cashier asked, "Cash or credit?"

The Lone Star card always felt like a billboard flashing "poor" in neon letters.

Momma pulled that card out like it was gold, no shame in her game. Me? I held my breath and prayed no one I knew was behind me in line.

Once I made it out and started the slow push of the grocery cart back toward the apartment, a jeep full of boys drove by. One of them leaned out the window and shouted something I didn't catch. I flinched anyway, my stomach turning as I gripped the handle harder and pushed faster. I hated this part, hated the way I wanted to disappear under the weight of my own body and the plastic bags swinging from the cart.

When I finally got home, Momma opened the door like she'd been waiting for me. She always kept one eye out the window. She knew the world too well to ever let her babies wander too far unsupervised. I think part of her was always a little scared for us, for what she couldn't control.

She kissed me on the forehead, smiled like she didn't see the dread in my eyes, and pulled the bags from my hands with a kind of strength only mothers possess. She was glowing that day, even though I could still see the tiredness in her. She slung bags over both arms and told me to stop carrying them like a scared little girl. "Hold your arms out, baby. That's how you get strong."

I tried. I really did.

Later that week, one of Momma's friends offered to drive me to the store. I thought I was off the hook from the cart-pushing misery, so I said yes quickly. She waited in the car while I grabbed a few things.

I noticed him before I heard him. He was tall, older, maybe even grown. He followed me from the cereal aisle to frozen foods, muttering something about how I looked "real cute." My breath caught in my chest. I dropped the last item in the basket and ran through the checkout like my life depended on it.

I bolted out the doors and back into the car. "Go," I said, panic in my voice. "Just go."

Momma's friend looked at me like I was crazy, laughing like it was the funniest thing she'd seen all week. That's when I saw the jeep again. The same one. Slowing down. Following.

At home, I slammed the door behind me and told Momma everything. And once again, her friend couldn't stop laughing. "That's just a boy," she said, wiping tears from her eyes. "Girl, you fine. He just trying to talk to you."

"Talk to me?" I snapped. "I'm twelve."

Momma pulled me close, sat me down, and said, "Some things in life are going to change whether you like it or not. You better get used to it, baby, because this world don't wait for you to be ready."

I didn't want to get used to it.

I didn't want to live in a world where going to the store meant bracing for catcalls, where my own body betrayed me by attracting people I didn't want near me. I felt like I was walking around in someone else's skin, pushed into a version of girlhood that wasn't safe anymore.

School didn't help.

Even some of the boys I'd known since elementary started acting different. They'd whisper, pass notes, bump into me on purpose, stare too long. One of them even had the nerve to pull on my hoodie one day and say, "You really think you can hide all that?"

I pushed him so hard he hit the locker. Everyone laughed, and I pretended not to care. But inside, I was boiling.

I started wearing baggy clothes—hoodies, oversized jeans, layers. I covered up everything I could, hoping it would protect me. Hoping it would make me invisible again.

But no matter what I did, the world saw something I didn't want to give.

By springtime, it got worse. Older boys from around the neighborhood started circling the block on their bikes, popping wheelies and throwing out compliments like candy. Some men would whistle from cars. Others would stare as I walked home from school, their eyes moving over me like I was grown.

I'd get home, close the door behind me, and melt into the couch. I didn't feel proud. I didn't feel wanted. I felt like something had been taken from me. My childhood was being eaten away one stare at a time.

I didn't talk to Momma much about it. I think I was afraid she'd think I was doing something to attract it. But sometimes, late at night, I'd find myself curled up next to her, just needing to be held.

Sometimes I still just needed to feel like a little girl.

CHAPTER 10

New Arrival

Unfortunately, Reggie was still around, lurking like a shadow that never quite disappeared. But Momma was done with him, at least emotionally. She didn't talk about him much anymore and when she did, it was with the tiredness of someone who knew better but still had to live with the consequence. His title had been reduced to one word: "sperm donor." And that's all he was—no more, no less.

One day, Momma stood in the hallway mirror, gently cupping her belly and pushing it out a little. She turned side to side, then looked over at us and smiled.

"How would ya'll feel about having a little brother or sister?" she asked casually, like she was testing the waters.

I remember my heart leaping before I even answered. For years I had begged her for another baby. Bianca and I both jumped with joy. I squealed, and Bianca clapped her tiny hands and danced in place.

"Well," Momma said, chuckling. "You got it." From that moment forward, everything changed.

Momma began shifting the house around, purging clutter, rearranging rooms. She was creating space—not just physically, but emotionally too. She was preparing us, herself, and our lives for something new. Our little family was about to grow. We didn't have much but love always seemed to stretch wide enough to make room.

The chaos of Reggie had left some aftershocks but the worst of the storm had passed—at least for us.

But then came Trisha.

Trisha was the kind of woman whose life could only be described as broken, and not just at the edges. Reggie had tangled her up, got her addicted to crack, and now she was living on the fringes of existence, floating from place to place, never really landing anywhere stable.

But Saniya—her little girl—was another story.

Saniya was beautiful. Wide-eyed and brown-skinned, with a giggle that made you forget the mess she came from. And Momma… well, she just couldn't turn her back on a child.

"She's innocent," Momma said one day as she braided Saniya's hair. "Her momma might be a crackhead, but that baby ain't done nothin' wrong."

I never understood how Momma could show so much compassion to a woman who once slept with her man, but I was starting to realize Momma didn't operate out of pride. She operated out of heart.

Trisha would come crying to the door, high and shaking, eyes darting like a raccoon's. Sometimes she'd drop off Saniya and disappear for days. I watched Momma gently wash Saniya's little body, pick lice out of her hair, and wrap her in a towel like she was her own. She didn't complain. She just did it.

But not every visit was calm.

One day, Saniya sat between Bianca and me on the couch, squirming and complaining about her bottom itching. Momma took one look and knew something was wrong. When she called Trisha to ask what was going on, Trisha said flat-out, "She got the worms."

Momma's face twisted in anger. "Take her to the hospital, Trisha," she said. But Trisha didn't have insurance, didn't want to go. So Momma took her.

I sat with Bianca in the waiting room, watching Momma pace with worry. I couldn't believe someone would let their child get that bad, but Trisha didn't have that kind of conscience anymore. Crack had eaten it away.

From that day on, Momma made it a mission to check in on Saniya whenever she could. She'd pick her up, bathe her, braid her hair, and feed her. Sometimes she'd try to clean Trisha up too—help her shower, get her new clothes, even help her apply for rehab. But every time, Trisha fell back into the same hole. And every time, it was Reggie waiting at the bottom of it.

The last time I saw Trisha, she was sitting on our porch, high as hell, smoking crack out of a soda can while Momma made dinner for the three of us girls.

Momma stepped out and told her, "You can't disrespect my house like this."

Trisha burst into tears, yelling and tugging at Momma's arm. "You said you wouldn't give up on me!"

I could see the fury building in Momma's chest. She tried to walk away, but Trisha followed. That's when I stepped up.

I grabbed Trisha by the shirt, eyes locked on hers. "You heard her. Get the fuck out."

She looked stunned.

"I'm not scared of you," I hissed. "But I got a pregnant mother to protect, and you better not forget that."

Momma had to pull me off. Trisha stumbled back, shaking her head. "I ain't mean no harm," she said weakly. Then she left.

The next time we heard about Saniya, it was from Trisha's mama. The girl had a broken arm. That was the last straw. Trisha's mama took Saniya in and we never saw her again.

Momma cried the night she heard. Not just because of Saniya, but because some part of her still believed she could save Trisha too.

As her belly grew round and full, Reggie disappeared more. I was grateful. I didn't want him around when my little brother or sister arrived.

We moved into a new apartment closer to Granny's. It was quieter there. Cleaner. Life started to settle. Momma and I got closer than ever during her pregnancy. She'd call me her "belly buddy" and joke that I was her midwife-in-training.

One afternoon, she decided to teach me how to make meatloaf.

"Every woman need to know how to feed a family," she said, pulling out the seasonings. "Ain't no shame in that."

I perched on the counter, watching her belly sway as she moved around the kitchen. She was glowing. Exhausted, yes, but glowing.

As I shaped my tiny meatloaf beside hers, I daydreamed about the baby. I imagined holding him—or her—in my arms, wrapping them in a soft blanket and claiming them as mine. In my little fantasy, Bianca came up and tried to play, but I shook my head and teased, "Nope, this one's mine. Just like you took my spot, now it's your turn to move over."

I giggled at my own joke, and Momma looked at me with a raised eyebrow.

"You alright over there?"

I nodded, smiling, still trapped in my own bubble.

That's when the knock came at the door.

It was Trisha again.

She looked worse than ever—hollow-eyed and jittery. Momma walked her straight to the back room. I followed, close but hidden.

The voices rose. Then suddenly, Momma had her pinned to the wall, hands around her throat.

"I said, get the fuck out my face," she growled.

I stood ready. One foot on the floor, my knee pressing into Trisha's side, my fist cocked back like a slingshot.

"Try it," I dared her. "Touch my momma and I'll tear you up."

Trisha looked between us, stunned. "I'm just playin'," she stammered.

I wasn't.

Momma ordered me to let her go. I did.

Reggie showed up minutes later to collect her.

We never saw her again.

Soon, it was baby shower time. A baby boy and girl topper decorated the whipped-cream cake. It was chocolate inside—my favorite.

The living room filled with laughter, gifts, and balloons. Momma wore a radiant smile, her belly proud. She still wasn't sure if it was a boy or girl, despite the doctor's assurance.

"I'm tired of splits," she joked. "I need a little boy."

Bianca didn't care. She was too busy running around with cousins and tearing open presents.

That night, I asked for the cake toppers. Momma said yes. I set the little boy and girl on my dresser like a shrine. But a few days later, the boy went missing. I searched everywhere.

"It's a sign," Momma said, shaking her head.

But then, the morning of her delivery, I opened the closet door and there he was—right in the middle of the floor.

Eric.

She laughed when I showed her.

"Okay, Lord," she said. "You made your point."

Eric was born April 1, 1996. Five pounds, four ounces. A spring baby with deep brown eyes and a quiet curiosity.

We stayed overnight at the hospital. The nurse rolled out a cot for me and laid Eric in my arms.

He stared right at me.

"Look, Momma," I whispered. "He knows me. He knows I'm his big sister."

She smiled. "Another grown one. Tryna hold his head up already."

I rocked him gently, his tiny fists curled against my chest. In that moment, I felt something I hadn't felt in a long time: peace.

The next morning, they weighed him again. The nurse asked something about "meconium," and I just stared.

Momma grinned. "That's baby's first poop, baby." Oh.

We brought Eric home that afternoon. Bianca watched him with fascination.

But I claimed him.

I looked down at his little face, his impossibly small fingers, and I made a promise.

"I got you," I whispered. "Forever."

He wasn't just my brother.

He was a symbol of something new.

CHAPTER 11

Sixteen Years to Life

Eric's crib sat right beside the bed, and even though Bianca and I had our own rooms, we always slept with Momma. It just felt safer. Her presence was a shield, soft and warm like the blankets we snuggled beneath. I never questioned it—we simply belonged together.

But those last few weeks, everything started to feel different. Heavier.

Momma still got up early sometimes to handle things but I could tell even when she kissed our foreheads goodbye that something was off. She wore worry like it was stitched into her skin. Her smile came slower, and her eyes—those deep, beautiful eyes—hid something from us. But she still played the role. She cooked breakfast, braided Bianca's hair, and changed Eric's diapers with her usual love and grace. But I saw the weight on her. I knew. I always knew.

Then came the morning she asked us if we wanted to come with her.

It felt exciting at first. Like we were in on something important. She explained in simple terms that she was "in a little bit of trouble," but had some good lawyers on her side. "This ain't all on me," she said, looking at me directly. "It got a lot to do with Reggie."

I nodded like I understood, though I didn't—not really.

We got dressed together. She stood in her closet, holding outfits in front of the mirror. She pulled out a black mini skirt suit and asked, "What about this one?"

I wrinkled my nose and teased, "It's cute, but what about yo' booty?"

She laughed—a real laugh. Loud and full. "Yeah, I better not. No telling what kind of women might be in that courtroom lookin' at me crazy."

We both cracked up. For a moment, it felt like a regular morning.

She chose a navy pinstriped pantsuit with a soft baby-blue blouse tucked underneath. I gave her a wink. "You gon' be fly," I said. She smiled wide.

I did Bianca's hair while Momma got Eric ready. Then Granny pulled up and honked from the parking lot. We piled into the car like we were headed to Sunday service, not court.

The drive felt long. Like we were being carried toward something we couldn't turn back from.

The courthouse was a big, brown-brick building with tinted windows that stared down at us like judgment itself. As we walked inside, Momma and Granny were met by two white men in suits—twins, apparently. One was big with a soft belly and strawberry-blonde hair; the other was short and bald. I didn't like how they looked at us, like we were a side project they forgot about until this morning.

They led us to a room filled with people. A large wooden gate divided the space. On one side sat three men, the prosecutors, I later learned. On the other, Momma's lawyers. We were ushered to sit in the back.

Then I saw her.

Momma came through a narrow side door and took her seat next to the bald lawyer. She didn't look at us right away. Her face was strong. Still. She was protecting us, even from the truth.

"All rise," someone yelled. Everyone stood.

The judge walked in, a tiny old white man draped in a black robe with spurs on the back of his boots. He had sunken eyes and a cold presence. He barely looked at Momma when he sat down.

"You may be seated."

The trial moved too fast. People spoke in complicated words, trading blame like cards in a game. The men on the right pointed fingers. Momma's lawyers argued back. But none of it felt real.

Until the big lawyer pointed to us.

I saw his hand gesture in our direction, and my stomach twisted. Granny dropped her head, shoulders shaking. Bianca leaned into me, clutching my arm.

Suddenly it was over.

We walked out in silence. The stairs creaked under our feet like they, too, were weighed down by sorrow.

Back in the car, Momma and Granny talked quietly. I didn't say a word. I just looked out the window and wondered how this story would end.

When we got home, I finally asked. "What's gonna happen now?" Momma motioned for me to sit down.

"Remember when I told you I stayed at a hotel that night a year ago?" she asked.

I nodded.

"Well, Reggie rented a car and asked me to drive it to meet one of his friends. I didn't want to. I told him no. But… I did it anyway. I got pulled over. The cops found a little piece of a blunt in the ashtray and decided to search the whole car."

I was frozen. "Was that it? Just the blunt?"

She shook her head. "They found drugs. Stuff he'd stashed without telling me. I had no idea what I was driving."

"Did you tell 'em?"

"Of course. But the system don't care about the truth, baby."

I knew what that meant. Reggie hit her. I remembered the broken dishes, the blood in the bathroom sink. I didn't need her to spell it out.

"So what we gonna do?"

"We're gonna pray that they give me just a little bit of time."

"No time," I said firmly.

She smiled, and her eyes welled up. "Jaydah, I messed up. I gotta own that. I just pray God makes a way."

I couldn't say anything else. I walked to my room, collapsed onto the bed, and cried into my pillow until the fabric was soaked. I didn't want Bianca or Eric to hear. I didn't want to scare them.

That weekend we tried to live like everything was normal. We had Sunday dinner with family. Momma took a long bath while Eric babbled from his crib and Bianca played with dolls. Even Dee called from California. That was rare.

Sunday night, Momma got us ready for bed. She held us close, let us stay up a little later. Bianca was glued to her side, dragging her feet when it was time to settle down. I told myself I was going to sleep in my own bed that night. I was nearly thirteen. A teenager. Junior high was just two weeks away.

I lay under my covers and stared at the moonlight slicing through the blinds. I tried to let it calm me, lull me to sleep. But the nightmares came fast.

Eric's furniture floated in the air. I saw an evil shadow laughing at me. I woke up in a cold sweat and ran for Momma's room, the hallway stretching like a tunnel.

I jumped into bed behind her. The gospel channel was still playing on TV, casting flickering light across the walls. Momma had prayed over the house before bed—shouting, crying, anointing every doorway with oil. Bianca and I followed her, mimicking her steps, echoing her cries. Even Eric joined in with his tiny baby wail.

Now, in the quiet light of the television, I saw something— a blur near the screen. My heart froze. My breath caught. But then I felt it: peace. A warmth wrapped around me like a blanket.

I heard my own voice whisper in my mind: *Everything's going to be okay.*

I closed my eyes and slept.

The next morning, Momma kissed my cheek.

"Go back to sleep, I love you, okay? Take care of my babies."

I nodded groggily. "I love you, too."

I didn't know, as a free woman, those would be her last words to me.

When I woke up again, Bianca was holding Eric, tears streaming down her cheeks.

"Momma's gone!" she sobbed. "She said she's not coming back!"

Eric wailed. I snatched the phone in her hand.

"Hello?" My voice cracked.

It was her.

"Jaydah, baby… Momma's not coming home today." My heart shattered.

"I need you to call your Granny in two hours. She knows what to do, okay? Be strong. Don't cry."

She hung up before I could speak.

I sat in silence. My eyes didn't blink. My hands trembled.

The room felt like it was closing in.

No mother.

No answers.

Just me and two tiny faces looking at me, needing something—*anything.*

I made a promise to myself right then: I would take care of them. I didn't know how. But I would.

I waited the longest two hours of my life and then called Granny.

She picked up with a gentle voice. "This is gonna be a very trying time, baby, but we'll make it through."

She said we'd pack a few things and stay with her. She said she'd figure it out.

I hung up, dressed Bianca, cleaned Eric, packed a bag, and walked. Granny only lived a few blocks away, but that walk felt like a lifetime.

I held Bianca's hand in one and Eric in the other. I was twelve years old but I felt like a mother already.

Granny opened the door before I could knock. Her eyes were red but she smiled.

"Come on in, babies," she said.

She didn't mention Momma. She didn't have to.

That night, I lay in Granny's guest room on a borrowed pillow soaked in tears. I stared at the ceiling and whispered Momma's name over and over like it was a spell. I thought about her laugh. Her advice. The smell of her skin. The feel of her hand rubbing my back when I cried.

And I realized something: Momma's sentence wasn't just hers.

It was mine too.

Sixteen years to life.

That's what they gave her.

But it felt like that's what they gave me, too.

Who was I supposed to become without her?

How would I survive?

I was just a child.

And yet I already knew… childhood was over.

CHAPTER 12

Three Children, Three Roads

The next morning, I woke up to the loud, overlapping voices of my aunts. It sounded like an argument. Five of them crowded around Granny's kitchen table, debating our fate like we were pieces of furniture to be divided up. I didn't want to hear what they were saying, but I couldn't tune them out.

"I'll take Jaydah."

"No, she can stay with me."

"I'll take the baby."

"Bianca's around my kids' age, so she can go to school with them."

Then another voice, cold and sharp, cut through the chaos.

"Hell, just send 'em to a foster home."

My heart dropped. I laid frozen on the upstairs bed, every muscle tense. I thought we were staying in our home. Momma was only supposed to be gone for a little while. I hadn't really let it sink in—what it all meant. But now I knew. They were splitting us up. Just like that.

I bolted toward the bed, climbed under the covers, and squeezed my eyes shut like it would make the world disappear. Like if I just slept hard enough, when I woke up, I'd be back in our apartment, Momma in the kitchen humming a song, Bianca begging for juice, and Eric fussing from his playpen.

But I couldn't disappear.

They were coming up the stairs.

I heard the creak of each step under their weight, the hush of their voices as they reached the top. They stepped into the room. I could feel their presence even through closed eyes. Someone shook my shoulder gently.

"Jaydah... baby, wake up."

I didn't move.

Another voice said, "Get up now. Y'all need to come downstairs."

Bianca stirred beside me. Eric was already gone—passed around like a baby doll downstairs, everyone cooing and claiming him like a prize.

Wendell's voice came next: "Should I tell 'em?" Granny answered softly, "No, I will."

We were led to the living room and made to sit next to Granny. She took a deep breath, her eyes soft but filled with pain.

"Your momma's not coming back, okay?"

I nodded slowly. Beside me, I could feel Bianca's shoulders shake. She began to cry quietly, the tears darkening her jeans, falling into her lap like raindrops on concrete. I gripped the edge of the couch cushion so tightly my fingers ached. I couldn't cry. I had to be strong. I had to be what Momma asked me to be.

"She's gonna be gone for a while," Granny continued. "Y'all are gonna live apart for now. But when your momma comes home, you'll be back together again."

I wanted to scream.

Why can't we just wait together? Why do we have to be separated too? Isn't it enough that she's gone?

"When will she be back?" I asked, barely above a whisper.

"A couple days? A few weeks?"

Granny hesitated. Her voice cracked. "Baby, your momma's gonna be there for years."

That word—*years*—hung in the air like smoke, choking me.

"What about our home?" I asked. "We can stay there, right?"

Shay jumped in, annoyed. "Ain't nobody got money to be paying for that apartment. And Momma sho don't."

My fists clenched in my lap. They talked about our home like it was just a lease. But it was our sanctuary. It was our story. Our safe place.

"Well look," Shay said, standing up like she was ready to leave, "I ain't got all day. Jaydah, you and Eric gonna come with me. You can stay at your same school 'cause I work out here."

Rita added, "Bianca, you'll stay with me. I got kids your age. You'll fit right in."

I stared at Bianca. Her lip quivered. My heart did too. We weren't just losing Momma. We were losing each other. Our voices, our little squabbles, our bedtime routines. She wouldn't be calling my name every five minutes anymore. She wouldn't be asking for my juice, my snacks, or begging to sleep in my bed.

We were being torn apart.

That night, as we loaded into separate cars, I watched her through the window. Her voice echoed in my head. "Momma, Jaydah won't gimme none. Momma, Jaydah won't let me play." I remembered the sound of her feet running after me, her laugh, her tears, her sticky hands clinging to mine.

Now she was crying for me and I couldn't do anything about it.

But I remembered Momma's last words to me. *"Be strong.*

Don't cry."

So I didn't.

Shay promised I'd see Bianca tomorrow. She said we just had some things to take care of at the apartment.

Sleep didn't come easily. I lay in a strange room in a strange bed in a strange house. Eric cried softly in the other room, and Wendell was there, holding him, patting him like he was hers. I could hear Fish playing cars on the floor, their laughter floating down the hallway like salt in an open wound.

I wanted to scream. I wanted to kick down the walls and put my family back together.

But I was too young to do anything but wait.

The next morning, the smell of pancakes and syrup crept through the house. I rubbed my swollen eyes and walked into the kitchen. Wendell saw me and motioned toward the bathroom.

"Go wash up," she said.

I stared at her, nodding, then turned and walked down the hall. The bathroom mirror didn't show me the same girl anymore. My eyes looked older, my face was tight and tired. I splashed water on it anyway, brushed my teeth, and walked out.

At the kitchen table, everyone had a seat except me. Wendell played with Eric, cooing and singing. Fish grinned and whispered, "Momma said y'all my family now."

I wanted to slap him. But I just rolled my eyes and stared at the table.

Wendell called out, "Fix your own plate."

She served herself and Eric and headed to her room. Fish trailed behind. I sat at the table alone. I cut into the pancakes slowly, each bite harder to swallow than the last. Tears welled up and fell quietly onto my plate. I didn't wipe them. I let them fall.

If Momma were here, we'd all be eating together. She'd be joking, dancing, making up silly songs with syrup in her hair and flour on her apron. But this was my new normal now.

After breakfast, I went back to my room and got ready to see Bianca. I picked out the least-ugly thing Shay had bought me. I stepped into the shower, let the hot water scald my back. My shoulders shook but I didn't make a sound. I sat down in the tub, holding myself, pretending it was Momma holding me. My tears mixed with the water and ran down the drain, taking pieces of me with them.

Just as I was beginning to calm, Fish started banging on the door.

"Hurry up! You takin' too long!"

I yelled back, "Wait!"

I heard his feet stomping off, then Wendell's voice down the hall.

"You got five minutes. Get out and get dressed."

I turned off the water and mimicked her under my breath.

Later, we all climbed into the car and headed to Aunt Rita's. When we arrived, Bianca came running. Her arms wrapped around me before I could even unbuckle. Shay and Granny were on the porch. Rita stood at the door.

I heard them talking about us like we were a burden. Like picking us up was an inconvenience. They were mad Momma left them with this responsibility, like we were some mess she made and disappeared from.

Did they ever think about what it felt like to be us? To be ripped from the only life we knew? Did they ever ask themselves if they'd trade places with her? Momma would've taken in any of their kids if it had been the other way around. She would've done it without hesitation. I knew that.

Bianca and I slipped inside, away from the grown folks' bitterness. We didn't play with the other kids. We didn't laugh. We sat close, understanding each other in silence.

Eventually, Aunt Rita came inside and said we were going to our apartment to get some more clothes and toys. My heart jumped, but all I really wanted was for us to go home—not just visit.

I asked if I could ride with Bianca. She said no. No room. I watched Bianca ride away in one car while I was stuffed into another. Separated, again.

Shay's car was a circus. She blasted old-school music and sang along, shouting lyrics like "I'm Every Woman" and "I Shot the Sheriff." I leaned against the window and tuned her out.

When we pulled into the complex, my breath caught.

Home.

Even just seeing it again made my heart ache. Everything looked exactly how we'd left it. The doormat was still crooked. The plants were still dying on the patio. The window in my room still had the little crack in the corner.

Inside, the air smelled stale but familiar.

I walked through each room slowly, memorizing everything. I didn't want to forget.

Rita said we had one suitcase. One.

I helped Bianca pick her clothes. We packed the toys she loved most. We didn't say much. We didn't have to.

Then I looked into Momma's room—and my blood froze.

Shay, Rita, and Wendell were laughing, standing in Momma's closet, trying on her clothes like it was a game. Picking out outfits. Claiming things.

I wanted to scream. *She's not dead. She's still our mother.*

That's not yours.

They called for us to come on. I noticed Aunt Dye outside loading furniture into her truck. Everything was disappearing.

I walked through the house one last time and remembered the egg sandwiches, the surprise gifts, the days she'd play music and spin us around. I remembered the time she made squirrel and I refused to eat it. The lemon-scented air freshener she always used. The way her laughter filled a room.

Now there was nothing but silence.

Shay yelled, "We gotta dump some of this. It ain't all gone fit."

I followed her outside and saw them breaking furniture, stomping on things, shoving them into the dumpster.

"That's my momma's!" I yelled. "Why you breaking our stuff like that?"

Shay barely turned around. "Yo momma ain't here. And don't nobody want this cheap shit anyway."

Tears burned in my eyes.

Our toys. Our memories. Our life.

Gone.

I looked at Bianca. Her face said it all—confused, sad, helpless.

They tossed everything. Picture frames. Baby books.

Drawings. Everything Momma ever saved for us.

"Ain't nowhere to put it," they said.

But they had homes. They had closets. They had everything.

And we had... nothing.

They packed what little they wanted into a storage unit, locked the door, and drove off.

I never saw that storage again.

I never saw most of our things again.

And just like that, our family, our memories, our childhood, was gone.

CHAPTER 13

Strangers with My Blood

School was in two weeks and I was depressed.

Not the kind of moody, pre-teen sadness that made you roll your eyes or pout because summer was ending. I was *hollow*. Like my chest had caved in and left nothing but silence behind. Usually, this was the time when Momma and I would be shopping for new clothes. She always said, "Out with the old, in with the new," even if we could barely afford it. It was her tradition. One pair of new jeans, two cute shirts, and a brand-new pair of sneakers—just enough to help me walk into a new school year with my head high.

This year, Momma was gone.

Instead of shopping with her, I was stuck trailing behind Aunt Shay in some dingy, fluorescent-lit place called Giddies Warehouse. It smelled like cardboard and cheap detergent. The racks were packed with outdated, scratchy clothes, and everything felt like it had been touched too many times by too many hands.

I picked up a pair of jeans I actually liked—tight enough to make me feel like myself—and held them up to my waist.

Shay took one look and snatched them out of my hands. "Uh uh. Too tight," she snapped. "You need room to grow."

If it had been Momma, she would've smiled, nodded, and said, "Those got a little sass to 'em, but you can pull it off." But Shay didn't want sass. She wanted me to disappear.

I grabbed a couple of t-shirts—nothing flashy—and still, she complained.

"All them colors too bright. You don't need to be drawing no attention to yourself."

She tossed three giant, plaid jumper dresses into the cart. Church dresses. Ugly ones. Ones that looked like punishment.

"I don't need no church clothes," I mumbled.

"You need what I say you need," she said, smiling like she'd won something. "You better be happy, 'cause yo momma sho didn't leave you nothing behind."

That comment sat in my chest like fire. My ears burned and I had to bite the inside of my cheek just to keep from saying something I'd regret. I wanted to slap the taste out her mouth. But I didn't. I waited until she turned her back and rolled my eyes so hard it hurt.

When we got back to her house, I dragged the bags inside and went straight to my room.

The house itself wasn't bad. It was big—a four-bedroom with a large den, dining room, and two bathrooms. But it was old, so old the floorboards creaked like they were whispering secrets at night. The kind of old where you could feel the stories in the walls. The kind of old that made you certain somebody had died in it.

Shay didn't even live there full-time. She stayed in an apartment up the street, five minutes away, and used the big house like it was a drop-off station. A place to park the kids.

Aunt Wendell and her son Fish stayed in one of the bedrooms. Their room was so small that the queen-size bed and dresser practically touched and Wendell couldn't even use the bottom two drawers. I was given the room next to them. It was slightly bigger but the closet was stuffed with someone else's clothes, like even the space didn't want to make room for me. I had to shove those clothes aside just to hang up the hideous jumpers Shay bought.

I could hear laughter drifting down the hallway. Wendell and Shay were saying their goodbyes. Their kids were crying, begging to stay the night together. It was a full house—full of people with my blood, but none of them felt like family.

From my room, I could hear Wendell cooing to Eric.

"My little baby," she sang. "My sweet boy."

Then Fish chimed in. "Momma, what's Eric gonna call you?"

"He can call me whatever he want."

"What if he wanna call you Momma like I call you?" "That's fine."

"Him and Jaydah my new brother and sister, right?" "Yes, they are."

"So they should call you Momma."

Then I heard it: "Momma Wendell."

My blood boiled. Momma hadn't even been gone long, and they were already trying to replace her. Like she was a position that needed filling. Like love could be reassigned.

I lay there that night, eyes wide open, listening to them laugh and play in the room across the hall. The joy in their voices made me feel sick. It sounded like a family—our family—but I wasn't included. And it wasn't real. It was stolen.

The next morning, I confronted Wendell. "Why you telling Eric to call you Momma?"

She looked at me over her glasses, unfazed. "Now, Jaydah, every baby needs a mother figure in their life."

"But he *has* a momma."

"Ain't nobody trying to erase your mother, girl. But you gonna stop this mess right now."

I knew when to shut up. I wasn't in a position to argue. But I made myself a promise. Eric wouldn't forget Momma. Not if I could help it.

That afternoon, while he napped, I slipped into Wendell's room and scooped him up. He barely stirred. I carried him into my room, laid him on the bed, and pulled out a picture of Momma. I sat beside him, pointed at her face, and said, "Momma. Momma. Momma." Over and over again, like it was a chant. Like I could etch her into his memory by sheer force.

Eventually, he pointed at the picture and whispered, "Momma."

I broke down crying. Silent, grateful tears. He knew.

He *knew*.

Then the door swung open. Wendell stood there, eyes narrowed.

"What you doing in here?"

"Showing my brother a picture of our mother."

She didn't say anything at first. Just stared. Then her mouth curled into a smirk.

"Your sister's on the phone."

She snatched up Eric, her frown disappearing into a wide grin as she kissed his cheeks.

I grabbed the phone before she could change her mind. I didn't even get the receiver to my ear before I heard Bianca sobbing.

"Jaydah, Chad punched me in my back."

"Did you tell somebody?"

"I told him I was gonna tell Momma, and he said our momma ain't never coming back."

I clenched the phone tighter.

"Don't listen to him. He stupid. Tell him I'mma knock him upside his head."

Bianca kept crying, trying to explain everything between gasps. I told her to stay strong. To call me if anything else happened. That night, I knew I was the only one left to hold us together.

The next day was my last day of summer. I begged Wendell to let me see Bianca. She agreed. Around lunchtime, she dropped me off at Aunt Rita's.

Carmen met me at the door with a half-hug. She was Aunt Rita's only daughter—pretty, with sandy red hair and light skin. Two years younger than me but already carrying herself like she ran the house.

Bianca saw me and ran. "Jaydah!" she screamed, wrapping her arms around my waist. "Are you going to get Chad for hitting me?"

"I can't just hit him, Bianca. But if he tries anything while I'm here, I'mma bust him upside his head."

Carmen rolled her eyes and flopped on her bed. I stared her down, then turned back to Bianca.

We snuck off to the bathroom for some privacy.

"When Momma coming home?" she asked.

"I don't know," I whispered.

I hated that answer. Hated I couldn't give her something real. Something solid. She looked up to me. I was her protector. If Momma wasn't around, she counted on me to be the one who knew things.

"She coming soon," I said, forcing a smile. "You won't be here forever."

She dropped her eyes. "Aunt Rita said she ain't coming home."

"She wrong," I snapped. "Don't listen to her."

Bianca's voice got quieter. "Yesterday, Carmen kicked me out the room. She said I cry too much. Then she broke her china doll and blamed me. Aunt Rita whooped me twice.

Once for crying. Once for saying I was gonna tell Momma."

My heart sank. I was trying so hard to believe that we'd be okay, but every story like this pulled me further down.

"Has she done that before?"

"Yes. Every time I cry or say I miss Momma. Every time."

I looked at her, all small and scared and trying to be brave, and felt rage rise in me like water boiling over.

"Don't let them see you cry," I said. "Be strong. You hear me?"

Chad started pounding on the bathroom door. "Get out!" "I'm talking to my sister, fool!" "I don't care!"

I swung the door open, still holding Bianca's hand. "If you put your hands on her again, it's gonna be trouble."

He laughed. "I'll hit you, too."

He stepped closer, but I didn't flinch. Just stared.

"Try it," I said.

He walked off, muttering under his breath.

Back in the room, Carmen and Bianca started playing with Barbie dolls. Chad came storming in again, accusing someone of breaking one of his toys.

"I ain't break your stupid toy," Carmen said.

"Well, somebody did!"

He slapped her.

Before I knew it, I grabbed him by the back of the shirt and tossed him against the wall.

"Leave her alone!"

Carmen ran to the bathroom, came back with a razor, and chased him down the hallway.

"Carmen!" I shouted. "Put it down!" "I'm tired of him hitting me! I'll kill him!"

"Carmen, he ain't worth it!"

She dropped the razor, slammed the door to her room, and locked it.

I sat on the floor, shaking. Bianca crawled into my lap, her arms wrapped around my waist. I didn't cry. Not in front of her. I held her close and promised—for the hundredth time —I'd protect her. That we'd make it through this. That Momma would come home.

When Wendell came back to pick me up, Bianca and I didn't cry. We didn't say much. We just hugged. Strong. Silent. Brave.

I gave Chad a look that said everything I couldn't say aloud.

And then I got in the car and turned my face to the window while Wendell sang gospel off-key the whole way home.

I thought about Momma.

The only people who were supposed to protect us had become strangers with my blood.

LETTER FROM MOMMA

21 September 1996

Hey, my Sweet Baby,

Mommie's ok. You all will be able to visit now. They have moved me to where I'll be staying until I come home. I love getting "Funky" letters from you. I'm going to write to you once a week and send you envelopes so you can write back to me, too. I know Aunt Wendell drives you crazy, but she is funny. Tell her hello and ask her to write to me. This place is a trip. Kiss Eric on his naked mouth for me. I know he is bad to the bone. I'll be home, so don't worry. Keep praying and I will, too. I'll write you again soon. I want some pictures of you, hear me!!! =)

Hugs and Kisses,
Soul of my Soul , Momma

CHAPTER 14

The Girl Who Didn't Belong

The first day of school was supposed to be a fresh start. New notebooks. New shoes. New homeroom. But nothing about that day felt new to me.

It was the start of seventh grade. I didn't want to be seen. I didn't want to be known. I wanted to crawl under a rock— or better yet, disappear completely. My body was there, walking through the hallways, sitting at the desk, pretending to listen. But my heart was still in that courtroom. Still clutched to Momma's dress when they took her away. Still trapped in a world that had shattered without warning.

The one saving grace was that most of my old elementary classmates hadn't been split up. Our school fed into two different middle schools, so there were just a few familiar faces sprinkled through the sea of strangers. I gave those few friends fake smiles when I saw them. Weak ones that didn't quite reach my eyes. I didn't want them to see the difference in me—the change in clothes, the quiet in my voice, the way I never quite looked anyone in the eyes anymore.

I used to be outgoing. Loud even. A little bossy. The girl who always had something to say.

Now I barely spoke.

Everything felt tight—my chest, my throat, even my jeans. They weren't new. Nothing I wore was. I kept pulling down my sleeves and tugging at the hem of my shirt, trying to disappear into the fabric. The other girls walked past me in shiny shoes and matching backpacks, laughing like life had never punched them in the stomach.

I sat through every class that day counting the minutes. I kept my head down. Answered only when called. Smiled when I had to. Laughed when it was expected. The whole day felt like I was playing a part in a play I didn't audition for.

I couldn't wait to get back to my room and hide away.

When the final bell rang, I didn't rush out. I sat on the steps out front, my backpack beside me, watching the other kids reunite with their families. Cars pulled up. Moms rolled down windows and shouted names. Kids ignored them the first time—just like they always did—but by the second or third call, they were waving goodbye to their friends and heading off.

I sat there, quiet, legs drawn in close. I reached into my bag and pulled out the two letters I had packed that morning. Both were from Momma. Both smelled faintly like cherry blossoms, a fragrance she'd normally spray her letters with. I unfolded the first one gently, smoothing out the creases, and read slow. So slow. I wanted to stay in her words as long as I could.

The world around me blurred. The voices, the footsteps, the exhaust from the buses. None of it mattered.

I just needed her.

When I looked up, most of the kids were gone. I saw Shay's car pulling in. She didn't have to call my name. I was already up, brushing off my pants, sliding the letters carefully back into my bag like they were made of glass. I climbed into the passenger seat and placed the bag in my lap.

Shay liked to talk a lot. Mostly about her sorority, her job, her plans. She never asked how I was doing. Not really. She didn't ask about my feelings or the letters or the weight I carried in my small, tense shoulders. She'd sing along to whatever gospel CD was playing, tapping the steering wheel with acrylic nails that clicked in rhythm.

The drive home was about 45 minutes. Long enough to sit with my thoughts but not long enough to sort through them.

After school, we always picked up Eric and Alex from daycare. I lived for that part of the day. I loved walking through the door and seeing Eric's whole face light up, his little legs kicking with excitement in the baby swing, his tiny hands reaching for me like I was his favorite person in the world. In that moment, I felt like I mattered. Like I belonged to someone.

Eric always had something new going on. One week, he was babbling new sounds. The next, he had learned to clap. Every little change made my heart ache. I knew Momma would be devastated to miss all of it. She always said babies grew too fast, and now she was missing it— every milestone, every new tooth, every giggle.

I'd pack up his daycare bag, zip his coat, and carry him out to the car. He wore this little puffy bodysuit coat that made him look like a snowman, stiff and round. He could barely move in it, and I'd laugh as he grunted with frustration trying to turn his head. Those tiny moments— those few seconds of joy—were what I lived for.

When we got back to Wendell's, she came out to meet us. She'd scoop Eric up in her arms and kiss his cheeks, her voice going soft and sweet.

"I missed you, baby boy."

I grabbed the diaper bag and my backpack and headed inside, straight to my room. I didn't linger. I didn't make conversation. I had homework to do but mostly I just wanted to be alone.

The house smelled like dinner. Shay and her sons were still in the kitchen, their voices blending in with the sound of pans and laughter. I finished my homework, then took a nap, retreating into sleep the way some people retreat into books.

That was my life.

That was my rhythm.

School. Wait. Letters. Carry Eric. Nap. Homework. Eat.

Sleep.

Rinse and repeat.

Thanksgiving came and went like a blur. Momma wrote to say she might be home by Christmas. She told me to pray about it. I did. I prayed every night. Begged. Bargained.

Believed. She said she might be released early. That her charges were false. That maybe, just maybe, they would send her home for the holidays.

Wendell, surprisingly, got into the holiday spirit. She pulled down old decorations from the attic. Put on Christmas music while she hung garland over the fireplace. Bianca and I helped her put up the tree but my heart wasn't in it. The lights twinkled, but they didn't feel magical.

We'd never had a Christmas without Momma. I refused to believe this would be the first.

I wrote Momma a letter and asked if they would let her go free for Christmas. Told her I missed her. Told her that she had to come home because it wouldn't be Christmas without her.

She wrote back gently. Said prison didn't work like that. Said she couldn't just come home for the holidays like it was a school break. Said she hoped, but she wasn't sure. Said, *"Just keep praying, baby."*

My birthday was five days before Christmas.

I didn't care about turning thirteen. I didn't want cake. I didn't want balloons. All I wanted was for the letter that came that day to say she was coming home. It didn't. She told me she loved me. Told me she was proud. But there was no mention of a release date. No hint this Christmas would be different than the rest of that god-awful year.

I felt like I was running out of time.

I wrote her again. Told her to remember what she said. Told her she promised. I dropped the letter in the mailbox and stared at it until the carrier came. I knew it took three days for letters to reach her. There was still hope. There had to be.

Christmas Eve came fast.

That day used to be my favorite—the gathering at Granny's house. All her kids. All the cousins. Laughter. Food. Too many people packed into too small a space. But this year, it felt like a play I didn't want to be in.

Everyone kept hugging me, Bianca, and Eric. Saying how sorry they were. How strong we were. How proud Momma would be.

It didn't help. It made me angry.

I wasn't some little orphan. I was just a girl waiting for her mother to come home. I didn't want sympathy. I wanted her.

Bianca cleaned up that year. Present after present pulled from under the tree had her name on it. Most of them were clothes. Things she needed. I figured Aunt Rita had made a list and sent it around. It was the family's way of feeling like they were doing something. Like they were helping.

I didn't care.

All I could think about was how split up we were. Bianca lived with Rita. Eric and I were at Wendell's. Nothing was the way it used to be.

After dinner, I climbed the stairs to the guest room and lay on the bed, staring at the ceiling fan as it turned slow, slow, slow.

She wasn't coming.

I had known it for a while. But still, the knowing felt different than the feeling.

She missed my thirteenth birthday.

She missed Christmas.

That night, I made another promise to myself: *Don't ever get your hopes up again.*

When her letter came a few days later, I didn't even want to read it. But I did.

She said she thought she'd be home. She said she was sorry. She said the charges were a lie. She said they couldn't keep her forever.

She signed it like she always did—*Soul of my Soul*—the song she always played for me when she cleaned the house. The one she'd spin around to, holding me in her arms, pressing my cheek to her stomach while we danced on lemon-scented floors.

I cried when I read it.

Then I folded it neatly, placed it in my box of letters, and sat up straight.

Her love—written out in those words—had to be enough.

For now.

New Year's came and went. I don't remember celebrating. I don't remember anything except the ache. Spring break was around the corner, but I didn't care. I didn't want birds chirping or flowers blooming. I didn't want sunshine or soft songs. I didn't want hope.

I wanted it all to end.

The sadness had started to harden. And beneath it was rage.

I hated the judge.

Hated the lawyer.

Hated whatever system thought it was okay to take a mother away from her kids.

I hated my aunts, too. Their smug looks. Their backhanded comments. Their way of reminding me I was the problem, that we were the ones dumped into their lives like stray dogs. If they could've sacrificed me like in one of those old Bible stories, I knew I'd be the first one on the altar.

I thought about Hester Prynne. The woman from The Scarlet Letter. Forced to wear an "A" for adultery.

I wore a "B."

B for bastard.

That's what it felt like. That's how they treated me. Like I was some cursed child. Some stain on their reputation. And I carried that weight like it was sewn into my skin.

Days stopped being days. I measured time by events.

School. Letters. Holidays. Visits.

And now the family reunion was coming up.

Another reminder, another public stage where I'd be the girl whose mom was in prison. The girl who didn't belong.

And once again, I'd be expected to smile.

LETTER FROM MOMMA

28 September 1996
The day I got your letter.

Hello Jaydah,

Mommie got your letter, and I was so glad to hear from you. I read them over and over again. I also sleep with them sometimes. Thank you for the picture of Bianca and Eric, but where is the picture of you? Keep Bianca in line and ask why she got kicked out of school. I hear that Eric is crawling now. Don't let him scoot out the door =) Granny and my lawyer are working on things. They say that I could be home by New Year's. Eric is so cute. Granny says he has two teeth now, top or bottom? I'll see when you guys come visit; looks like he is getting fat, too. Well, Jaydah, my brown-eyed girl, Mommy loves you. I have to go now, but I will write you again soon. Have to wake up to work in the field. We are like human lawn mowers, weed eaters, and rock crushers. Don't be scared when you come to visit, this place is very different than home. Just remember, I love you, and send me a picture of yourself. I'll be home, hopefully, for our birthday. Lots of kisses and hugs to share with Bianca and Eric.

Luv Always Momma

CHAPTER 15

Letters and Lullabies

Life on the outside kept moving.

Bianca was stringing words together like she had something to prove, sometimes to herself, sometimes to me. She'd follow me around the house, dragging her little blanket like it was a part of her body, sometimes calling it "Momma" and tucking it into her shirt like she was carrying a baby too. She had her own language for comfort.

Eric, on the other hand, had just figured out how to escape. Crawling like he was running from something, always darting under tables or slipping behind cracked doors. His giggles sounded like wind chimes, soft and surprising. His laughter would echo in the hallway, bouncing between rooms like joy trying to find a home. Their lives kept unfolding like chapters in a book I had no hand in writing. I just flipped the pages, trying to keep up.

They were changing every day.

Somehow, I wasn't.

The moment Momma went to prison, it was like the world pressed pause on me. Everyone else hit play. Growth, joy, pain, learning: they passed through Bianca and Eric like sunlight through a window. But me? I just… sat in the dark. I was there, sure. I went to school, I bathed, I brushed my teeth. But I didn't breathe the same. I didn't laugh the same. The girl I'd been when Momma was home vanished like vapor.

Wendell's house didn't help.

It was neat and tidy, sure. It had structure. But it didn't have warmth. There were no smells of dinner cooking, no music playing from the radio like back in the day. No yelling from Momma telling us to "cut that mess out before I come in there!" It was silent, but not peaceful. It reminded me something was missing, someone.

I stayed in the back bedroom. Mine, technically. But it never really felt like mine. I never put up posters. Never threw clothes on the floor just to be messy. I kept it clean, quiet. Like a guest.

Like I wasn't sure how long I'd be allowed to stay.

I'd sit on the edge of the bed, swinging my legs like a child who couldn't reach the floor. Watching shadows from the blinds stretch and shrink across the carpet, my thoughts crawling even slower than the clock.

I wasn't waiting for someone to play with.

I was waiting for the mail.

Because Momma's letters were my everything.

When they came, the world cracked open just enough for the light to peek through. She decorated the envelopes with stars and little hearts like she was tucking love in all the corners.

Each envelope was more than paper. It was a portal.

Her letters weren't just updates. They were lullabies. Confessions. Prayers. When I read them, I wasn't in Wendell's house anymore. I was with Momma—braiding her hair, standing in the kitchen licking cake batter off a spoon, curling up on the couch while she rubbed my back until I fell asleep.

I memorized her handwriting. The way her letters leaned slightly left. The way she dotted her "i" like she was making sure she didn't forget even the smallest thing. I'd trace her words with my fingers, whispering them out loud like scripture. On bad days, I'd fold them back up and slip them under my pillow, pressing my face against the cotton like her love could seep into my skin.

Some nights, it felt like it did.

But letters, no matter how precious, couldn't erase reality.

I still had to hand Eric over every night. Fish and Wendell made their claim, and I didn't argue. I didn't know how. I just kissed his soft cheeks, breathed him in, and handed him over. Sometimes he'd reach back for me. And sometimes he didn't.

And that stung.

Wendell's room was across the hall. At night, I could hear them laughing. Not loud. Not wild. Just… comfortable. Like a family. The sound of a bedtime story. A small joke. A soft goodnight.

And then there was me, curled in a comma under stiff sheets, listening from across the hall like a ghost in my own life.

Sometimes I'd whisper to the ceiling, pretending it was the sky. "Tell her I'm trying," I'd say to the stars. "Tell her I miss her."

There was no phone I could use. No Instagram feed to numb the ache. Just silence. Silence and the creaking floors. Silence and the rustle of Bianca in her sleep. Silence and my own thoughts, screaming.

On better nights, I'd draw. I made pictures for Momma. I'd sketch her in a big pink dress, surrounded by flowers, holding Bianca and Eric like she had never let go. I drew a house with curtains and a porch swing. A place we could live again. A place we could be whole.

I never mailed those.

I kept them in a shoebox under my bed like wishes I didn't trust the world to handle.

Then there were the lullabies.

I made them up for Eric, silly little things about clouds and rocket ships and peanut butter sandwiches that fly. I'd sing them while giving him his bath, letting him splash while I scrubbed behind his ears. The songs didn't rhyme right, and didn't always make sense. But he'd giggle like I was the funniest person in the world. I sang to him like Momma used to sing to me. Even if he wouldn't remember, I needed to believe the sound of my voice, the care in my hands, would leave a mark.

Sometimes I caught Bianca humming them too, rocking her blanket-baby to sleep, singing something soft and off-key. That little girl carried more heart than most adults I knew. She didn't need much—just a lap to curl into and someone to listen when she babbled her stories about stars and clouds and what her imaginary cat did that day.

One night, she asked me, "Do you think Momma dreams about us?"

I paused.

"All the time," I told her.

She nodded like she already knew the answer but needed to hear it out loud. Then she laid her head on my lap and said, "I dream about her too."

We sat like that in silence. Two girls in a world that didn't feel made for us, clinging to lullabies and letters like life rafts in a storm.

But not every night was quiet.

There was one night—cold, with the windows sweating on the inside—when I heard Eric crying in the other room. A sharp, startled cry, not his usual whimper. It made my heart race. I got out of bed and opened the door, but Fish had already picked him up. He looked over at me like I had overstepped, like I didn't belong in that hallway, like I wasn't his sister.

I hated that.

I hated how the world around me had redrawn all the boundaries of what love was supposed to look like. I hated how people who had barely held him as a baby now rocked him like he was theirs.

But more than anything, I hated how I let them.

Because I didn't know how not to.

I didn't have a plan. I didn't have power. I didn't even have a voice most days. Just a room, some paper, and a box of drawings I didn't know what to do with.

So I wrote Momma back.

I told her everything. Every tear. Every joy. Every quiet betrayal. I filled pages with confessions and prayers and questions I knew she couldn't answer.

One letter, I wrote:

"Do you still know me?"

Another:

"Will we ever be a family again?"

She never gave me direct answers. She didn't promise a fairytale ending. She couldn't. But she did something else. She gave me glimpses. She wrote about how she was teaching how to do hair—tight cornrows, box braids, slicked buns.

She talked about the women she met. Some had no visitors. Others had children who stopped writing. She said every time she saw a child come for visiting hours, it made her ache. But when she got a letter from me, it made her feel like somebody again.

"I'm more than my number," she wrote. "I'm your Momma."

And I'd whisper that to myself on the hardest days.

She's more than her number. She's my Momma.

Then I'd pick up my pen and write back.

One afternoon, I came home from school and the mail was late. I paced by the window, chewing my nails, feeling the panic start to rise in my throat. What if she stopped writing? What if she gave up? What if something happened?

Then I heard the mailbox creak.

I ran so fast I scraped my shin on the coffee table.

Inside the envelope was a single page. No decorations this time. No stars. No perfume. Just her words:

"Jaydah, I need you to know something. You're my reason. Every day in here, I think about your face. Your strength. Your heart. I don't want you to carry me. Just remember me. And keep going."

I sat on the floor with the letter in my lap, the sunlight hitting it just right so the words shimmered through my tears.

I didn't cry hard. Not that day.

I cried soft, the kind of cry that sneaks out through a smile.

Because for the first time, I didn't feel invisible. I felt seen.

I wasn't just her daughter.

I was her reason.

That night, something shifted.

I didn't float through the evening like a ghost. I didn't lay in bed counting the cracks in the ceiling, waiting for sleep like a punishment. I moved. Slowly, yes. But deliberately. I reheated leftover spaghetti and made Bianca a little bowl with her favorite plastic fork—the one with the faded cartoon handle. I gave Eric his bath and didn't rush it. I let him splash and shriek. I sang to him until his giggles melted into yawns.

When Fish came to get him, I didn't hesitate. I kissed Eric's cheek and handed him over with steady hands. I didn't ask for more. I didn't beg. I just whispered "I love you" and watched him go.

Then I went to my room, pulled out my sketchbook, and drew Momma.

But not the usual version—the one behind bars, or in her green prison uniform, or the sad-eyed woman I remembered from the last visit. I drew her free. Hair twisted up in a headwrap, big earrings, arms wide like she could hold the whole world. I drew her standing tall with Bianca holding one hand and Eric the other. And I drew myself, too—next to her, not behind.

When I finished, I stared at it for a long time.

It wasn't just a picture. It was a hope I hadn't dared to name.

A better future.

Ours.

Sundays were the loneliest. Church mornings brought everyone into a whirlwind of motion—pressed clothes, quick breakfasts, car rides filled with gospel humming or the occasional fuss about someone being late. I always felt like an extra in someone else's film. Not the star. Not even a supporting role. Just there. Present, but fading into the corners.

This Sunday was no different. Fish and Wendell went early. I stayed behind with Bianca, who was fussy because I wouldn't let her wear her princess costume under her dress. She cried big, dramatic tears that only stopped when I let her wear the plastic crown.

"You look beautiful," I told her.

She sniffled. "Like a queen?"

"Exactly."

After church, we came back to the house and everything felt routine. Bland food on heavy plates. Conversations that skirted around me. I took Bianca outside while she played with chalk on the sidewalk. She drew stick figures and suns with long eyelashes. I sat on the stoop and opened another one of Momma's letters.

This one was longer than usual.

She talked about a program she joined that helped women prepare for life after prison. They were teaching job readiness, budgeting, even how to parent again.

"I don't know if I can do it," she wrote, "but I want to try. For you. For them. For me."

Those words caught me.

For me.

Not out of guilt. Not just survival. But because she wanted more for herself too.

Maybe that's what real growth looked like. Not perfection.

Just wanting more. Trying, even when it hurt.

I folded the letter and looked at Bianca, who was now covered in chalk dust.

"You hungry?" I asked.

She nodded. "Can we make pancakes?" It wasn't morning, but I said yes anyway.

We made a mess in the kitchen—flour on the counters, syrup on the stove. I cracked the eggs wrong and she dropped one on the floor, laughing like it was the funniest thing she'd ever seen. It wasn't perfect. But it was ours.

For the first time in a long time, I felt like I was part of something again. Not just surviving or waiting, but actually living.

That night, I tucked Bianca into bed and laid down next to her for a little while. Her crown was crooked on the nightstand, glitter barely hanging on. She turned over and wrapped her small arm around my neck.

"Tell me a story," she said.

I hesitated.

"I don't know any stories."

"Make one up," she whispered.

So I did.

I told her about a girl with a soft heart and a strong spine, who carried her family in her arms and dreams in her pockets. Who learned to build homes out of broken things. Who sang lullabies that stitched the sky back together. Who found her way back to love, one letter at a time.

When I finished, she was already asleep.

But I kept talking anyway, because maybe the story wasn't just for her.

Maybe it was for me too.

Letters kept coming.

So did the small moments that kept me going.

Like when Bianca learned to tie her shoes and screamed through the house like she had discovered fire. Or when Eric said "Jay-jay" for the first time and even though he probably didn't know what it meant, it still felt like he had called me home.

I kept drawing.

Kept reading.

Kept writing to Momma, not always about pain but sometimes about joy too.

And slowly, I realized I was changing.

Not all at once.

Not in the ways people could see.

But inside.

My spirit was stretching. My heart was learning how to hold more than grief. I wasn't healed. But I was healing. There was a difference.

One day at school, I raised my hand in class. Just once. Just to answer a question I knew the answer to. My voice was shaky, but it was mine.

At lunch, I sat with a girl named Tamika who asked if I liked poetry. We traded notebooks for the afternoon and promised to write something new the next day.

At night, I still whispered to the stars.

But now I added something new.

"Thank you," I'd say.

Thank you for getting me through another day.

Thank you for letters and lullabies.

Thank you for Momma.

LETTER FROM MOMMA

23 October 1996

Hello My Beautiful Baby,

Mommie got your letter and picture. I was glad to hear from you and very happy to get a picture. Please, send more. I will write to Rita and ask her to ensure that you see Bianca every weekend. Jaydah, Granny and I are working hard with the lawyers to try to get me out of prison. Please keep praying for the Lord to set me free. It just takes time. Yes, baby, I will be home before 2000. I love you so much, and yes, my baby, I remember and miss the times we played together, slept in my big bed, and ate all kinds of junk, looking at TV all night. Yes, you can pick me a husband, but I'm not looking. I want to spend time with my babies to make up for the time I'm spending here. You, Bianca, Eric, and Dee are my world; I live for you guys. If I didn't have you to come back home to, I couldn't make it. You, my precious, are my reason to keep fighting for my release. I know sometimes I was hard, and maybe it seemed like I didn't care, but I've always loved you. Jaydah, I know you will always be there for me. You've always been strong, just like me. I've gotta go to sleep now, breakfast is at 3:45 a.m. Kiss your brother and sister for me, and here is a big kiss for you.

Hugs and kisses,
Love always Mommie

PS You are the Soul of my Soul.

CHAPTER 16

Visiting Hours and Vending Machines

Visiting Momma was never just a visit. It was a ritual.

It started the night before. Granny would gather me, Bianca, and Eric like a general preparing her troops. Her house was always warm, smelling of wood polish and that old fabric softener she'd been using since before I was born. Something about the creak of her hallway floors made everything feel more stable. We knew what to expect there. Her predictability made us feel safe.

She didn't fuss. She didn't explain. She just moved around the house with a kind of quiet urgency, laying out our clothes, setting our shoes in line by the door, and making sure Bianca's hair was neatly braided. Eric's bag was packed with only what was allowed. Diapers. A bottle. Wipes. No toys. No extras. The rules had no room for softness.

That night, Granny didn't say much. She didn't need to. Her silence was heavy with meaning. It said: "Get ready." It said: "Be strong." And, somewhere under all that: "I wish this wasn't our life."

We always left before the sun came up. By five a.m., we'd be in the car, the windows fogged, the streets still dark. Granny never played music on those drives. She kept both hands on the wheel, eyes forward, her mouth drawn into a tight line. It was like the closer we got to the prison, the less oxygen there was. The silence wasn't peaceful. It made your chest hurt.

By hour three, my stomach would be in knots. I'd recognize the trees that lined the road to the prison. The vast nothingness that surrounded it. The parking lot looked the same every time: gray, cracked pavement and worn yellow lines. And the building itself? All concrete, metal, and wire. It looked like punishment. Like someone had taken all the warmth out of the world and sealed it behind steel doors.

The line to get in was always long.

People stood with toddlers on their hips, diaper bags on their shoulders, eyes full of something that wasn't quite hope. Some families whispered to one another. Others didn't talk at all. It felt like we all shared a secret pain no one outside those walls could understand. A kind of grief that never really ended, just paused between visits.

Check-in was cold and meticulous. A guard would wave us through the metal detector one by one. Bianca knew how to stand with her arms out, how not to flinch if the wand beeped. Eric's bag would be opened, turned inside out, examined like it might hide a weapon instead of wipes. Granny's purse—clear and carefully packed—was always searched. Tissues. ID. Mints. That's all she ever carried.

Once cleared, we were sent into a waiting room with plastic chairs and gray walls. A television mounted in the corner played the same three channels. No one paid attention to it. We were all watching the hallway.

Waiting for her.

When Momma appeared, it never mattered how tired we were. Bianca's eyes lit up first. She'd whisper "there she is" under her breath, as if saying it too loud might break the moment. My heart would catch in my throat. Eric would start bouncing in my arms like he knew something important was about to happen.

She always came out with her chin up.

Even behind that uniform, even under those harsh fluorescent lights, she carried herself like she wasn't broken. She'd smile the moment she saw us. Sometimes, she made silly faces through the glass to make us laugh. She always found a way to bring softness into a place that tried to strip it away.

When the door finally opened and she stepped into the visiting room, it was like the air changed. That first hug? It healed something every time. She'd hold us like she was trying to glue all our broken parts back together.

"My babies," she'd whisper, burying her face in our hair.

For the next three hours, we became a family again.

There were no toys. No play area. Just cold chairs, a few vending machines, and lots of rules. We weren't allowed to leave our seats for too long. Eric had to stay calm. Bianca had to stay quiet. I had to stay composed.

Still, we found ways to make the most of it.

"Granny, can I get something from the machine?" I'd whisper.

She'd pull out a handful of quarters and nod. Every visit, it was the same snacks: honey bun for Bianca, sour cream chips for me, grape soda to split. When the vending machine worked—it didn't always—it felt like a small win. A red coil spinning out a package of comfort. If it jammed, we'd just stare at the glass, willing the snack to fall.

Momma never ate much. She was too focused on us. She held Eric like he was still a newborn, whispered in his ear like he could understand every word. She smoothed Bianca's hair and asked about her dreams. When she looked at me, it was always with a kind of reverence, like she saw more than just her oldest child. Like she saw her anchor.

"You're doing good, baby," she'd say. "You're stronger than I ever was."

Her praise felt like sunlight. It warmed me in places I didn't even know were cold. I needed to hear those words. I needed to believe I was holding it all together, that all the effort and silence and swallowed tears meant something.

Those three hours moved fast.

The last thirty minutes always came too soon. We'd fall into silence again, stealing glances at the clock, holding tighter to her hand, her shirt, her voice. It became harder to smile. Harder to talk. The goodbye hovered long before it was spoken.

"Five minutes," the guard would call out.

That's when Bianca would break. Every time. She'd sob into Momma's shirt, gripping her like she could stop time. Eric would start to fuss, sensing the tension. And me? I'd try to stay tall. To swallow the lump in my throat. To be the brave one.

"Be strong for me," Momma would say, kissing us one by one.

And we'd nod, even though we were already unraveling.

The final hug hurt the most.

It was never long enough. Never soft enough. Never enough to last us until the next visit. We'd cling to her until the guard stepped forward, and then we had to let go. We always had to let go.

As we walked out, the air felt heavy again. Granny didn't speak. Her steps were slower. She always paused near the gate, looking back like she might change her mind, like she might storm the place and take her daughter home.

But she never did.

Once in the car, no one talked. We sat in silence. The sadness rode with us like a fourth child. Eric would fall asleep first, then Bianca. I'd stare out the window, trying to memorize the shape of Momma's smile, the sound of her laugh, the way her hands felt when they held mine.

Somewhere along the drive back—usually near West, Texas—Granny would break the silence.

"We're stopping," she'd say.

Her sisters lived there. Aunt Sue. Aunt Nettie. Aunt Lila. Women with loud voices and open arms. They didn't ask too many questions. They just loved us. They fed us, kissed our foreheads, and let us be children again. No rules. No guards. Just warmth.

Aunt Lila would pull me into the kitchen and show me how to season chicken without using a measuring spoon. "Feel it in your bones," she'd say. "Your hands will know when it's right."

In those moments, I felt connected to something bigger than myself. Something ancient. Something that survived even this.

We'd return home full of food and stories.

But as the days passed, the distance between visits stretched like a rubber band—always tight, always threatening to snap. I marked the calendar with invisible ink. I memorized the days since our last visit, counted the days until the next.

The older I got, the more rules changed. At twelve, I could no longer sit on her lap. At thirteen, our hugs were timed. By fourteen, we had to sit across the table, separated by a line we weren't allowed to cross.

Momma's face didn't change. Her love didn't shrink. But the system tried to make our love small. It tried to turn visits into transactions.

We didn't let it.

We turned vending machine snacks into picnics. We made games out of counting the buttons on the guard's uniform. We told stories. Shared secrets. Prayed with our hands linked under the table.

It was never enough.

I'd leave the prison holding every "I love you," every "I'm proud of you," every stolen smile like treasure in my pocket. I'd hold them until the next time.

Visiting her was both wound and balm.

It reminded us what we'd lost—but also what still remained.

It was in the early goodbyes and the long drives back. In the scent of grape soda and pressed clothes. In the strength of a grandmother who refused to let her daughter disappear into the system. In the resilience of children who still believed in hugs and honey buns.

It was our way of holding on.

It was the only way we knew how.

And as long as she was in there, we'd keep going back.

Every few months. Every three hours. Every vending machine miracle.

Every ritual of love inside a place designed to erase it.

LETTER FROM MOMMA

6 November 1996

Hey Jaydah,

I wanted to let you know that I am ok. I know this looks like a really bad place, but there are ladies here just like me, mommies waiting to go home to their children, too. I go to work and go to church; I'm waiting to go to school. Jaydah, Momma will be home in 1997, I can't tell you when, but don't you worry. Just help Aunt Wendell take care of Eric. Call Bianca; I know she misses you a lot. You have to be there for her since I can't be. Just remember, honey, Momma will always, always love you, and these people can't keep me here forever, and no, you won't have to spend 16 years with Aunt Wendell. Anyway, my baby, I know you need me, my prayers and thoughts always have you in them. You are my reason to live. Write me back soon. I miss your letters.

Hugs, Kisses, and lots of Love,
Momma

PART III

NO ONE TOLD ME I WAS GROWING UP

A childhood over before it truly begins

CHAPTER 17

Big Sister

The morning after the reunion, I woke up still emotionally raw. The curtains were drawn just enough to let in a streak of pale sunlight, the kind that didn't warm, just illuminated. My pillow was still damp from the tears I'd cried the night before. I moved quietly, not wanting to see or be seen, not by Wendell, not by Fish, not even by Bianca, though I longed for her the most.

The ride back from the reunion had been long and too quiet. Bianca fell asleep somewhere between West and the freeway entrance, curled up beside me, her breathing soft and steady. Wendell drove with both hands on the wheel, her eyes fixed ahead. Eric sat behind her in his car seat, chewing softly on the ear of a stuffed dog.

That picture, us standing alone, looped in my mind like a scene I couldn't escape. No one said anything afterward, but I felt their eyes. Felt the weight of their silence. It wasn't just that they made us take that photo without Momma, it was that they expected us to smile like we weren't broken.

At home, Wendell handed me a foil-wrapped plate and told me to eat. I nodded, placed it in the fridge, and went to my room. I didn't even change. I just laid down, the dark swallowing me whole, and pulled the blanket over my head.

I didn't cry right away. I tried to hold it in. But when I heard Eric stir in his sleep, a soft sound from the other room, the tears came quietly, soaking into the fabric of my pillow. I didn't want anyone to hear. I didn't want anyone to come in and ask what was wrong because I wouldn't have known how to answer.

I wasn't the only one hurting. Bianca was too little to fully understand, but I saw it in the way she looked at the door like she expected Momma to walk through. And Eric, he was still a baby, he wouldn't remember any of this. But one day, he might ask about that photo and I'd have to tell him what it felt like to stand in front of our whole family without the person who mattered most.

Still, I never thought of myself as the only one holding everything together. My Aunts were not the most affectionate but they came together to take care of business.

Wendell, Shay, and Rita managed the logistics, school forms, meals, and getting us from one place to the next on a daily basis. Granny filled in the cracks, taking us to see Momma, driving us back and forth between Wendell's and Rita's to see each other, and praying more than speaking. Others stepped in when they could, sometimes cold, but trying in their own way. Even Aunt Dye, in her distant manner, was part of the mix. The adults were doing what they thought needed to be done.

But while they managed the schedules, I managed the silences. The looks. The questions that never got asked. The ache. I learned to see what no one said.

Being the big sister didn't mean being the mother. It meant being the one who saw it all and chose to stay.

The next weekend, I asked Granny if I could stay with Bianca. We hadn't spent time together. Aunt Rita wasn't very proactive about dropping Bianca off at Wendell's. She met the minimum, meals, a bed, clean clothes, but no affection. She didn't smile when she saw us. Didn't speak more than a few words. She never made me feel like I was welcome, just tolerated. Bianca never reached for her hand or sat close. And Aunt Rita didn't offer softness back.

When I knocked on her door that Saturday, she opened it with her usual clipped expression. "She's in the back," she said flatly, stepping aside without a word of greeting.

"Thanks," I mumbled, walking in with my bag.

Bianca was sitting in the hallway, legs crossed, coloring in the margins of an old notebook. Her face lit up when she saw me. She ran and hugged me around the waist like she hadn't seen me in years.

"I missed you," she said softly.

"I missed you more."

Aunt Rita didn't say anything as I helped Bianca get her bag ready for the night. She handed it over and turned away before I could say goodbye.

That night, back at Wendell's, we built a tent out of bedsheets and string lights. It wasn't fancy, but it was ours. Bianca laid her blanket close to mine on the floor. We whispered about silly things. If we could live in a candy store, what kind of candy would we eat forever? If we had a house shaped like a crown, what color would we paint the roof?

And then the laughter settled. The quiet crept in.

After she fell asleep, I laid awake, my eyes fixed on the ceiling, listening to her breath. I didn't feel like a mother. I didn't want to be a mother. I was still trying to be a child. But I couldn't stop caring. I couldn't pretend I didn't feel her sadness, or my own.

The summer moved slowly. The days were hot, sticky, and often uneventful. I spent more time in my room, where I escaped the stress of life through books. I read books about girls who survived impossible things. Stories about mothers and daughters who found their way back to each other.

And sometimes, I wrote.

In a notebook I kept under my bed, I wrote small entries.

Quiet confessions.

"Today I remembered the way Momma used to laugh. I miss that sound."

"Bianca asked if she could sleep in my bed again tonight. I said yes."

"I don't think anyone sees how hard I try."

At Wendell's, nothing changed dramatically. She had her system, tight schedules, strict rules, and little space for softness. But she kept us going. I suppose that was her way of showing love.

Still, what I longed for wasn't structure. It was Momma's presence. Her warmth. The sound of her voice humming in the kitchen. The sight of her dancing in slippers. I missed her in all the places she used to be.

There were days I wondered what it would be like to forget. To stop holding onto the ache like it was my last connection to her. But forgetting felt too dangerous, like losing her all over again, so I remembered everything, even when it hurt.

Back-to-school season arrived too fast. Eighth grade loomed. I wasn't ready - not because of the academics but because seeing girls with their mothers reminded me of what I was missing out on with mine. I'd never gotten my nails or toes done with my mother. I'd never been to the mall with her to shop. Hell, I'd never even sat next to her in a movie theater.

Every family gathering that summer reminded me I was different. No one said it directly. But I saw it in the pauses. In the way people glanced at me when I entered a room. In the way they praised me for being a "little lady" but never asked what it cost.

I remember one afternoon at Aunt Nettie's house. Everyone was eating ribs and baked beans off paper plates. I sat under a tree with Bianca while Eric napped in Wendell's lap. A cousin asked if I took care of them by myself.

"No," I said.

He raised his eyebrows. "Really? You always got 'em with you."

I forced a smile.

Later that day, Aunt Lila sat next to me on the porch. She looked at me long before she spoke.

"You remind me of your momma," she said. "Serious.

Watching everything."

I didn't say anything.

"She used to do that too. Carry too much."

It was the only time that summer someone really looked at me and saw the weight.

Being the big sister didn't mean being the parent. It didn't mean doing everything. It meant showing up. Being the quiet witness, the one who says, "Me too," when the pain gets too big.

I didn't know what my life would look like five years from now. Or ten. But I knew this: I would still be their big sister.

And that, no matter what, would always be enough.

LETTER FROM MOMMA

20 December 1996

On this special day, 13 years ago, God sent me a precious little angel I named Jaydah. That little angel grew into a beautiful young woman. I love that angel very, very much. I wish I were there to share this day with you, but my heart is always with you. I love you so much, I can't tell you enough. Take care of yourself, Bianca, and Eric. Lots of love and kisses for me, I'll be home soon. This is the first and last time we will be separated. Pray daily for everyone, including those who treat you poorly and say hurtful things. I may not be able to buy you anything for Christmas or your birthday, but I send you all my love, hugs, and plenty of kisses.

Luv Momma

CHAPTER 18

Echoed Laughter

Living with Wendell, most days passed in silence. Not the peaceful kind, but the kind that settles in your bones when no one asks about your day, when no one waits up for you, when your name is only called to hand over a chore or pass a message. Most days, it felt like I was renting space in her house, not living in it.

I didn't go to school with the neighborhood kids, which meant I didn't go outside much. I'd watch them from the window sometimes, bike races, sidewalk chalk, games of tag that stretched across front lawns, but I never joined. I was a stranger in the place I lived. Aunt Shay always cooked dinner, I'll give her that. Despite how I felt about her most days, she was consistent.

My life was built around a pattern that never changed: get up early, ride across town with Aunt Shay, catch the bus to Granny's, sit there for less than an hour, then get picked up again by Shay for the long ride back home. The days were routine. The pain wasn't.

By then, it had been two years since Momma left. Two birthdays. Two Christmases. Two summers. That's how I counted time now, by how many holidays she missed. The memories of when she was still with us weren't fading, but they lived deeper now, tucked under layers of sadness and time. Those long car rides with Shay were the worst. There was no music, no conversation, just my thoughts pressing heavy against the inside of my head. Sometimes I'd turn my face toward the window and cry silently, hoping she wouldn't notice. I didn't want her asking questions. I knew she wouldn't offer comfort if she did.

Summer days were mostly spent babysitting Eric, Fish, Alex, and Yella. The house was full of noise but none of it felt like it belonged to me. Fish and I clashed constantly. He was spoiled and loud, always needing something, and got it without question. Wendell treated him like royalty, ironing his socks, lining up his shirts perfectly in the drawer. He moved through life as if the world should center around him, and it did. Part of me resented how easily everything came to him. I gave him a hard time, maybe out of jealousy, maybe out of pain. But it didn't matter. Wendell didn't like it. She defended him every time. I wasn't her child, and she never let me forget it.

Sometimes, I'd wake up to Yella's high-pitched voice echoing through the hall. He and Fish would sneak into my room and throw toys at me before darting out, laughing. I'd sit up, groggy and annoyed, listening to their laughter trail off down the hallway. Eric would be on the living room floor playing quietly. Shay would be in the den, and Wendell would already be at the stove. It was a house full of people but I still felt like the loneliest person in it.

On good days, Shay tried to pull me out of the routine. She'd take me with her to the store, not for the company but because she knew I needed to get out of the house.

Sometimes during the drive, she'd talk to me. She'd mention her sorority and the wisdom of life. Her words never fully sank in but I appreciated the effort. I clung to any moment that made me feel like more than just another responsibility.

That day, we walked each aisle of the grocery store picking up dinner ingredients and items I'd need to make lunch for the boys the next day. I stayed close, pushing the cart, watching her move quickly from item to item. She didn't ask what I wanted. She never did.

When we pulled into the driveway, Fish and Yella were already outside. Wendell yelled her usual greeting from the doorway, and I stepped inside to put the bags away. I slipped into my room and fell backward onto the bed, my body heavy with exhaustion that had nothing to do with chores. I stared at the ceiling. Sometimes, I imagined growing wings and flying away from it all to a world where Momma was home, where I was allowed to laugh without guilt, where being a kid didn't come with so much pressure.

The dream faded fast when Wendell barged in holding a letter. "It's from ya momma," she said. She tossed it onto the bed without even looking at me. I waited until she left, then grabbed it quickly. My name was written in Momma's careful handwriting, the envelope decorated with little stars and a drawing of Mickey and Minnie Mouse. My heart lifted. It wasn't long, but it was her voice on paper, and that was enough.

I folded it gently and tucked it into the box under my bed. That box held my survival—every letter, every scrap of love Momma had managed to send from behind bars.

Later that afternoon, I made my way to the kitchen for a snack and drink. As I sipped from the cup, I saw Fish staring at me.

"You got my Batman cup," he said, already on the verge of tears.

"So?" I said. "There's more cups."

"But I don't want you drinking out of that one," he whined.

I rolled my eyes. "Too late."

He started crying, and within seconds Wendell stormed outside. "What you do to him?" she barked.

"Nothing. He wanted this cup, and I told him I was already using it."

"Give him the cup," she snapped.

"I'm drinking out of it!"

"I said, give it to him, now!"

I held it out and let it fall. The cup hit the driveway and cracked, juice spilling out. Fish wailed. Wendell's eyes went wide with rage. "Why you do that, Jaydah? Pick it up."

I picked it up in silence and walked inside. That's when I saw the letter, two pages, sitting on top of the TV. I glanced at it, recognizing Momma's name. It wasn't from her, though. It was addressed to her from Aunt Rita.

My stomach twisted.

Wendell stormed in behind me, belt in hand. "Oh, you think you too grown now?" she yelled. "Think you can talk back, break stuff, and do what you want?"

She raised the belt. I caught it midair.

Her face twisted in shock. "Oh, so you wanna fight me? Fight me then."

I backed away, but she came at me swinging. I could feel her weight slam into me, fists pounding. My mind went blank. I'd never fought anyone like this. Never raised a hand to family. But I couldn't just take it.

We wrestled, shoving, yelling. My head hit the wall. Her nails scratched my arm. I fought back. I didn't know what else to do.

Eventually, she stopped. Breathing hard, she stood over me. "Had enough?" she spat.

I didn't answer. I just looked away.

She walked off, and I walked over to the letter. My hands shook as I picked it up. The words hit like punches: accusations, judgments, insults hurled at Momma for the way we'd been raised. Brags about how they "saved" us, how they were fixing what she broke.

I folded it and hid it with my letters from Momma.

That night, I couldn't sleep. I stared at the ceiling and wondered if this was what growing up meant, learning to live with pain. I asked if Momma would read that letter and cry the way I did. I wondered if I'd ever feel like someone's child again, not just a body shuffled from one house to another.

The next morning was the first day of school. I got dressed in silence. Shay drove me to school. I kept my face turned to the window, hiding my swollen cheek and my tears.

The first bell rang. I stepped into the school hallway, backpack slung over one shoulder, shoulders squared. No one asked about my summer. No one noticed the sadness tucked behind my eyes.

But I was there.

LETTER FROM MOMMA

December 22, 1996

Hello, my Sweet, Beautiful Baby,

I hope my letter finds you feeling better. By the time this letter reaches your hands, Christmas will be over, but not the love of God or the love I have for my children. Jaydah pray for all the other children whose mothers or fathers are also in prison. I hope you understand that the greatest gift to receive on Christmas is LOVE, and not things. Things get old, we break them, and we lose them. Love never grows old; don't lose it, and it can't be broken. I got your love on Christmas Day. So, always give love, love God first, and try always to do good. I'm very proud of you for getting good grades. I knew you could. Here are the answers to the songs.

1. S.N.= Silent Night
2. P.I.N.A.P.T= 12 Days of Christmas, Partridge in a Pear tree
3. R. The R.N.R= Rudolph the Red Nose Reindeer
4. D through the S= Dashing Through the Snow

Please send me another puzzle, I loved it. Here is some paper for you, soul of my soul. Kiss Bianca and Eric for me

CHAPTER 19
School Days

We pulled up to Forest Meadow Junior High just before the morning bell rang. Aunt Shay didn't say much; she never really did when she dropped me off but this time even the silence felt different. Maybe it was the weight of another school year starting, or maybe it was just me. Either way, I closed the car door gently, barely catching her muffled "Bye" through the window, and walked toward the building.

The air was thick with chatter and excitement. I could hear laughter and greetings echoing off the brick walls. Some kids ran to hug their friends, others posed for pictures, their smiles wide and carefree. I tucked myself into the edge of the crowd, watching as group after group reunited like pieces of a puzzle finally snapping back into place.

I found a few of my old friends near the front steps, girls I used to laugh with at lunch, boys I'd once passed notes to in class, but it wasn't the same. Their voices didn't hold the warmth they used to. The hugs were brief. The conversation short. One by one, they drifted away like the tail end of a song. I guess they didn't know what to say anymore. I guess I didn't either.

It wasn't just that Momma was gone. It was everything that came after.

I stopped trying to explain myself. I stopped answering the questions that never got asked but always lingered in the air. I started walking the halls like a ghost—present, but not seen. I didn't want pity. I didn't want to hear, "I'm sorry" or "That must be hard." I wanted to forget long enough to make it through the day.

Dance class became my escape.

I signed up for it without thinking twice. It didn't matter what kind of dance. We did modern, jazz, hip-hop, a little ballet. I wasn't there to impress anyone. I just needed a place where my body could speak when my words couldn't. At first, I was stiff and unsure. I hadn't had formal training. But something about the music, the rhythm, the movements, gave me a place to exist freely. When I danced, I wasn't "the girl whose mom is in prison." I was just me. Moving. Breathing.

It turned out I had a natural feel for it.

By mid-year, the dance teacher, Ms. Kearns, pulled me aside and told me I had potential. "You've got presence," she said, "even when you're not trying." I didn't know what to do with that kind of praise. I shrugged and looked down, but a part of me clung to her words.

Dance practice also gave me more time at Granny's house. It was a quiet kind of peace. I'd stay there after school until Shay picked me up. Granny didn't ask too many questions. She just made sure I ate, and sometimes, that was enough.

I met two new friends, Tiff and Tamika, through dance. They were girls who liked to stay after class and stretch, sharing hair ties and snacks and whispering about crushes during water breaks. They didn't know about Momma. I never told them. It was easier that way. I'd laugh with them, even when it felt like a performance. I let them believe I was just another eighth-grader. And for a little while each day, I was.

But there were costs.

I used my lunch money to pay for dance shoes and performance clothes, to contribute toward costume fees and field trips. Most days, that meant I didn't eat. I got used to the hunger. I told myself I wasn't really hungry. I'd drink water until the ache went away and count the hours until dinner.

One of my friend's moms noticed. She pulled me aside after a school showcase and asked if I was okay.

"You're so thin, sweetheart. Are you eating enough?" I lied, of course. Smiled and said yes.

But that night, I looked at myself in the mirror and saw what she saw. My collarbones were sharp. My clothes hung off me. I started eating more, at night and in the morning before school, just enough to put some weight back on. I didn't want anyone else to notice.

I didn't want anyone to see me as broken.

And yet, I was.

Not because of what I'd lost, but because of what I couldn't fix. I couldn't bring Momma back. I couldn't make things better for Bianca. I couldn't stop the ache that followed me from class to class.

Boys started noticing me too, but I didn't understand why. My self-esteem was still buried somewhere under the shame. I didn't think of myself as pretty. I was the skinny girl with the light skin and quiet hazel eyes. The one who barely spoke in class and always turned down invitations. I didn't wear the trendy clothes. I didn't have a phone or money for snacks or after-school outings.

Sometimes the boys would linger in the hallway watching me.

"You got some hips on you," they'd say with lustful eyes.

"You tryna hide that body?"

I hated it. It made me feel seen in all the wrong ways. I'd tug my shirt down and walk faster, not sure if I was supposed to feel complimented or exposed. Aunt Rita used to tease me about my hips, like they were something to be ashamed of. I started believing her.

I learned to shrink myself. I sat small in chairs, avoided mirrors, wore baggy clothes when I could. The more invisible I became, the safer I felt.

Spring came fast.

Eric was talking more, walking like he'd always known how. He called Wendell "Momma" now, and every time I heard it, my chest burned. She let him say it, never corrected him. He didn't know better. He was just trying to belong to somebody.

I didn't blame him.

He was still my baby, even if he didn't know our history yet. I made sure to send Momma updates, letters filled with pictures and milestones, things I knew she was missing. I wanted her to feel connected. I wanted her to know we were still hers.

Bianca still struggled. I saw her when I could, but the visits were harder now. Aunt Rita was always frustrated, always yelling. Bianca was getting into fights at school. She'd come home with scratches, stories about being sent to the office. I tried to talk to her about it, but she shrugged me off.

"She said I was bad," she told me once. "Said I act like I ain't got no home training."

I wanted to scream.

Bianca was eight. She wasn't bad; she was grieving. But no one gave her the space to feel it. They only punished the outbursts without asking where they came from.

Weekends were the worst. Aunt Rita had this rule, "Every man for themself." She didn't cook. Didn't check in. Bianca had to fend for herself, find food, and stay out of the way. Sometimes she'd call me crying, asking what to eat. Other times, she wouldn't call at all, and I knew that meant she was trying to survive the weekend like it was a storm. She learned to cook ramen noodles and wash her own clothes fast.

I did what I could. I visited. I cooked when I could. I brought her books and helped her with her homework. But I wasn't a mother. I wasn't in control.

I just hoped she knew I was trying.

The worst part was how Carmen sometimes acted. She once told Bianca, "I've been more of a sister to you than your own sister." As if sisterhood were measured by presence and bullying. As if love could be proven through control.

Bianca never talked to me about our situation after that.

She shut down. Built a wall I couldn't get through.

I didn't blame her.

I felt like I'd failed her. I felt like I'd failed Momma too. She had told me to "take care of my babies," and I was doing everything I could, but it never felt like enough.

That spring, I turned to the Bible more than ever. Not out of obligation, but because it gave me something steady. I read the Psalms on quiet mornings, underlining verses that sounded like me. I wrote prayers in the margins. I asked God for strength, for clarity, for a little bit of peace.

I didn't get answers. But I got through the days.

That was something.

The rest of the year flew by. Ninth grade loomed ahead. People started asking about high school, what electives I'd take, whether I wanted to try out for the drill team or join the student council. I nodded along, pretending I was thinking about all of it, but in truth, I only thought about survival.

I kept the secret life I lived hidden behind decent grades and quiet behavior. No one asked questions. No one noticed when I stayed late at school to avoid going home too early. No one noticed when I sat alone at lunch, eating slowly, reading a book I wasn't really focused on.

I preferred it that way.

Telling the truth would mean exposing the raw, hurting parts of me. The parts that cried at night and felt invisible during the day. I didn't know how to ask for help.

I just kept going.

Dance became my safe space. Bible study became my anchor. Letters to Momma became my therapy. And silence became my survival.

School days weren't about learning. They were about pretending. Pretending to be okay. Pretending I wasn't afraid. Pretending that maybe, just maybe, things would get better.

LETTER FROM MOMMA

16 February 1997

Jaydah,

You know if I were home, I'd try to give you stars, the moon, and the sun, but I'm not there now. Will you please take all of my love instead? Here is a picture of the stars, moon, and sun; this will do until I can come home. Mommie will always be praying for you. Remember, each day or month means I'm closer to home, closer to being a family again. Don't worry, God and His angels are protecting me, and He is flying me on the wings of angels

Luv Kisses Mommie

P.S. Take care of Bianca and Eric

CHAPTER 20

Silent Rage

The summer of 1998 burned slowly and heavily. School had ended, and with it, any small distraction I had from the chaos and quiet storms I lived with. The air in Dallas stuck to your skin in the summer months and I felt like I was suffocating, not just from the heat but from everything I was holding in. There was something about that summer that etched itself deeper into me than the others. Maybe it was because I was about to start high school. Maybe it was because two years had passed without Momma, and I still couldn't figure out how to breathe right without her.

Fish and Yella had their schedules packed. Sports games, t-ball tournaments, weekend events. Aunt Wendell and Aunt Shay were always buzzing around making sure the boys had everything they needed: uniforms pressed, snacks packed, team pictures framed on the walls. At every game, I watched them cheer loud, beam with pride, high-five other parents like we were all part of the same picture-perfect family.

Except we weren't.

I sat on the bleachers with Eric, usually feeding him or trying to keep him entertained while the sun beat down. I'd glance at Wendell clapping for Fish, her smile wide, like nothing in the world had ever gone wrong. Shay would be bouncing Alex on her hip, offering juice boxes and coaching tips. I saw joy on their faces. Saw belonging. And it made the ache inside me even worse.

I felt like a ghost.

Most of the time, I moved around the house invisible. Unless Fish was crying about something or I used the wrong tone of voice, no one paid me any attention.

Wendell's priority was always Fish. Everything he wanted, he got. If he didn't want it, he got it anyway just in case he changed his mind later. She even ironed his underwear and socks.

After a long day of cheering Fish and Yella on at their T-ball game, we pulled into the driveway. I went straight for the bedroom without even take off my shoes. I looked on my bed and there it was: a small envelope with my name in her neat handwriting. I didn't even read it right away. I just held it to my chest and lay back, letting my body melt into the mattress.

It took me a few minutes to work up the courage to open it. My heartbeat sped up the closer I got. I read every word slowly, like I had to commit it to memory. It wasn't long, but it was warm. Momma had drawn hearts in the corners. I could tell she didn't know what to say, but I could feel her trying. That was enough. I folded the letter gently and slid it into the small box I kept tucked behind some books on my shelf. That box held pieces of her, the parts I still had.

I lay there for a while, silent tears tracing the edges of my face. I didn't sob. I couldn't. I had mastered the art of quiet crying over the past two years. Especially on those long drives with Shay, when the silence between us was heavy. I'd press my forehead to the window, let the cool glass soak up my sadness, and cry most of the way home.

Sometimes I wondered what it would feel like if someone noticed. If someone asked. If someone cared.

But no one ever did.

That night, I didn't eat. Shay came to the door with her usual tone, brisk and sharp, and told me dinner was ready and that we'd be going to visit Momma the next day. I nodded without answering. I didn't feel like seeing anyone, not even Momma. I wasn't ready to pretend like everything was okay when I knew it wasn't.

Later that night, I lay in bed staring at the ceiling. I could hear Wendell laughing in the other room with the boys. Her voice was so bright, like nothing about our situation was strange or sad. I hated that laugh. Not because it was loud. But because I couldn't remember the last time someone had laughed like that with me. I clenched my teeth. My fists balled up against the sheets. The rage inside me wasn't loud or explosive. It simmered beneath the surface, a steady boil I could barely control.

I couldn't take it anymore.

I slipped quietly into the bathroom and opened the cabinet under the sink. I didn't know what I was looking for. Pills. Razors. Anything that might make the pain stop, even just for a moment. I found a small razor tucked in a plastic case and took it back to my room. I closed the door behind me and sat on the floor.

The room was dark. Just a sliver of moonlight poured through the blinds.

I looked at the razor in my hand, then at my wrist. My skin. My life. I took a deep breath and dragged the blade across, just enough to feel the burn. It wasn't deep, but it stung like fire. I dropped the razor and buried my face in my hands. Tears fell fast and hard. I hated myself for doing it. I hated I felt this way. I hated no one saw me. No one knew.

But I also didn't want to die.

I just wanted someone to care enough to stop me.

The next day, I wore long sleeves even though it was hot. Shay didn't notice. Wendell told me that if I killed myself, the world would keep spinning. Not sure if that was her way of relaying it wasn't worth it.

We visited Momma that day, and I remember staring at her, wanting so badly to tell her about everything. To spill it all, the cutting, the sadness, the way I didn't feel like myself anymore. But I couldn't. Granny had made it clear. "Don't overwhelm her," she'd said. "She's got enough to deal with."

So, I smiled. I made faces with Eric. I told Momma about my grades and how I was going to high school soon. I watched her eyes light up with pride, and for a moment, I felt whole.

But the second we left the visitation room, the emptiness returned.

Summer dragged on. I kept to myself, wrote in my journal more, and found new places to hide my emotions. I cut a few more times when it got bad, but I also read my letters from Momma over and over. Those letters were the only thing that kept me anchored. They reminded me that someone still saw me. Still loved me.

Sometimes I imagined what it would be like when she came home. Would I be the same? Would I even know how to talk to her anymore? Would she be proud? Or would she see right through me?

I didn't know. But I hoped.

Hoped was the only thing I had left.

And even in my silent rage, hope was the one thing I hadn't let go of. Not yet.

One afternoon in late July, Wendell called me into the kitchen.

"Shay's got an appointment tomorrow," she said flatly. "You need to watch the boys."

I nodded. "Okay."

She narrowed her eyes. "I know you got your little moods or whatever, but I don't want no attitude. You hear me?"

"I said okay."

She turned away before I finished my sentence. I stood there for a moment, watching her stir the pot on the stove, the smell of greens filling the room. I wanted to ask her something, anything, like if she ever thought about what I was going through. But I didn't. I knew better by now.

Later that night, I sat in my room and pulled out my journal again. Writing had become the only way I could release the fire inside of me.

July 21, 1998

Dear Diary,

Sometimes I think I could scream, and this whole house would keep going like nothing happened. Like I'm not even here. Fish cries, and the world stops. I cry, and the world keeps moving. Am I invisible? Or do they just not care?

The next morning, I made waffles for the boys. Eric danced in his little pajamas and threw a piece of waffle on the floor. I picked it up and laughed a little. He looked up at me and grinned, syrup all over his cheeks.

"You silly," I said softly.

He reached out and hugged me around the leg. That small act cracked something open in me. I closed my eyes for a second and let myself feel the warmth, the simplicity, the reminder that someone still needed me, still saw me.

We played in the living room until Shay came back. She barely said anything to me, just mumbled a thanks and dropped her keys on the counter. I gathered my things and went back to my room.

That night, I had a dream I was back in our old apartment. Momma was on the couch, folding clothes. Bianca was at the table drawing and Eric was crawling on the floor. There was laughter. There was light. I woke up and stared into the darkness, the ache so real I could taste it.

July 24, 1998

Dear Diary,

I think healing might be slow. But I think maybe it's possible. Maybe one day I won't feel like I'm drowning in my own silence.

I decided to stop being so hard on myself and let myself feel everything. The grief. The fear. The longing. But also, the love. Because even through the rage, through the silence, through the ache of a summer that almost swallowed me whole, my mother's love will always find me.

LETTER FROM MOMMA

1 March 1997

Hello lady Jaydah,

I got your letter and Bianca's picture. I wrote to you a couple of days ago as well. I love you so much, and I miss you. I try not to worry about you, but I can't help it. I don't want anything or anyone to hurt my babies. I've hurt you guys enough by getting myself locked up in prison, but I pray and ask God to please send me home soon. You look so pretty in your picture. I know it's kinda hard living with Wendell. She is crazy. Shay is, too. You are mine, so you are strong and can hang in there until I get home. You are my sunshine; each and every one of you. Anyways, tell Shay and Wendell I said hello. Hope granny brings you to see me soon. Hugs and kisses, souls of my soul.

Love Mommie

P.S. BIG KISSES

CHAPTER 21

Barbed Wire

I woke up to Wendell yelling my name from across the house. Her voice pierced the morning air like a sharp slap, jarring me awake from a dream I could barely remember but didn't want to leave. I rubbed my eyes, glanced at the clock, and remembered, it was visit day.

We were going to see Momma.

I got up and stretched, my body still heavy from a restless night. I walked over to Eric's crib, where he was still curled up like a little bean, his breathing soft and even. "Time to get up, baby boy," I whispered, brushing my fingers across his cheek. He stirred, and soon his little arms reached up for me. I lifted him out, sat him on the edge of the bed, and started braiding his soft curls into neat cornrows. We had to look good. No, we had to look perfect, for Momma. She hadn't seen us in person in months.

I dressed him in his favorite overalls and a clean shirt. Then I threw on a denim skirt and blouse, nothing fancy, just neat. Something about preparing to see her made me slow down and pay attention to the details. Like if we looked okay, it would ease her pain somehow. Like our clothes could speak for the love we weren't allowed to express in full.

We piled into the car. Wendell had already packed snacks and water bottles for the drive, and Granny was expecting us. The ride to her house was mostly quiet. Eric babbled in the backseat, asking about biscuits and juice, pointing out passing cars. I answered him gently while Shay talked Wendell's ear off in the front.

When we got to Granny's, I saw Bianca at the window. She looked thinner, older somehow, and yet exactly like I remembered. As soon as we got out, she ran up to us and wrapped her arms around Eric and me. I held her tightly, pressing my face into her hair. I felt guilt sitting heavy in my stomach, guilt for not protecting her more, for not being there more. But I also felt relief. She was still my baby sister.

Shay and Wendell followed behind, talking about something petty, gossip that had nothing to do with what we were about to face. I ignored them.

Granny, as always, wasn't ready. She was still putting on her earrings and looking for her Sunday purse, the same one she always took when we visited Momma. She moved slowly, her body not as strong as it once was but her eyes just as sharp.

We finally got on the road. The drive took about an hour and a half but felt longer. Time bends when you're heading toward something you both long for and dread. Every mile closer made my stomach churn. The image of that barbedwire fence, the concrete walls, the steel gates— every detail branded itself into my memory every visit.

Granny had her rules. "Don't tell your momma none of that bad stuff, ya hear?" she reminded us from the driver seat. "Only good. She can't handle nothin' else." I nodded, even though I wanted to scream. How could we protect her from the truth when we were drowning in it?

We arrived and parked in the same lot, in the same spot, next to the same crack in the pavement, and the same security guard was behind the glass. The metal detector buzzed softly. The air inside the building was stale.

We sat in the waiting room for what felt like hours. Bianca fidgeted with the hem of her dress. Eric clung to my hand. Then, through the far glass door, I saw her.

A slim figure in prison whites, smooth brown skin that still radiated beauty despite the fluorescent lighting. She stuck out her tongue playfully. Bianca squealed, "That's Momma!" I smiled, but it ached. The joy was always mingled with a little sadness.

She came through the doors, arms outstretched, eyes shining with tears. We each got one big hug, one of the two I could receive during the visit. She picked up Eric, but he turned away from her. He looked confused and uncomfortable. His small hands reached back for me. Momma's face crumbled. She turned her back quickly, wiping a tear before it could fall. "It's okay," she whispered, her voice shaky.

She kissed our cheeks, gently, like she was afraid we'd disappear.

"Jaydah, you been a big girl? Taking care of my babies?" she asked.

"I do my best, Momma," I answered. But my throat was tight. I didn't want to cry. I needed to be strong for her, the way she needed me to be.

Granny immediately took over the conversation. Her voice was loud, firm. She talked about court hearings, parole rumors, the letters, the neighborhood. I sat beside Momma and just watched her. Memorized her face, her hands, the way her eyes lit up when Bianca talked about school.

I didn't really know the full story of why she was in prison. That day, I learned more than I ever wanted to know. The whispers started when Momma leaned in and said, "Jaydah, baby, I didn't know there was a gun in the trunk. I swear I didn't know." Her eyes searched mine for understanding.

"The prosecutors said I was runnin' drugs. Said I was a boss. Said I had a whole operation. But baby, I was just tryna survive."

She lowered her voice. "They wanted Reggie. He been runnin' from them for years. They tried to get me to talk. Threatened me with time. And he... he threatened me right back."

I listened, stunned.

"He said if I said a word, he'd start with Granny. Then Bianca. Then you." Her voice cracked. "He said he'd take Eric and raise him himself, so I kept my mouth shut.

A guard tapped her wrist. Time was up.

Momma stood slowly, gave us all one last hug. "I love you. Always, always love you," she whispered into my ear. I held onto her for an extra second before letting go.

We watched her walk back through the gate. Just like always, she stuck out her tongue from behind the glass window. It was her little signal, her way of saying, "I'm still here."

And then she was gone again.

We piled into the car and headed back to Dallas, silence filling the space between us.

Granny made her usual detour through West, stopping to see her sisters and check in. We stayed in the car mostly. Bianca was curled against the window, half-asleep, her lashes resting heavy against her cheek. Eric was already out cold in his car seat, his little fingers still clutching the zipper on his hoodie. I sat in the back, staring blankly ahead, letting my mind drift in and out of thoughts I couldn't hold too long without breaking.

By the time we got to Granny's house, it was already dark. Too late to drop us off at different homes, so we stayed the night. Her porch light buzzed as we carried sleeping bodies inside. Bianca rubbed her eyes and shuffled toward the couch. I scooped up Eric, his head heavy on my shoulder, and Granny opened the door for me. "Set him down gently, baby," she whispered, reaching for his blanket.

Granny handed us nightgowns and made us laugh with her usual teasing. "Y'all look like twins in them gowns. Just missing the ruffles and bows," she said, making Bianca giggle. It was one of the only times I saw Bianca relax. In those few minutes before bed, with Granny brushing her fingers through Bianca's hair, we were just kids again.

I laid down beside Eric and closed my eyes. For the first time in weeks, I slept like a rock.

When I woke up, the smell of bacon and fresh biscuits filled the air. Granny's kitchen was alive with noise—Uncle Junior talking loud over the news, Aunt Dye humming as she stirred grits on the stove. Everyone had their own place at the table. Granny poured juice into mismatched glasses and told Eric to come sit next to her. I fixed a plate for Bianca and handed it to her. She smiled a soft thank you and began to eat.

I took my plate to the kitchen when I was done and started rinsing dishes. Granny shouted from her seat, "I know somebody better wash them dishes too!" I turned around. Aunt Dye and Uncle Junior were both looking right at me like I was the dishwasher. I didn't complain. I scrubbed the plates, rinsed the grease from the pans, and wiped down the counters. No thank you. No help. Just silent expectation.

After breakfast, Wendell and Shay showed up to take us home. Wendell walked straight in and scooped up Eric, holding him up like Simba from *The Lion King* and kissing his face. "You miss

Momma?" she asked him sweetly. Her voice twisted the knife in my chest. It hadn't even been twelve hours since we saw our real momma. I wanted to scream: **You're not his momma.** But I stayed quiet. I always stayed quiet.

They chatted with Granny about the visit—what Momma looked like, what she said, what she wore. Then their voices lowered into hushed tones I couldn't make out, but I knew what was coming: gossip. Schemes. Lies to tell Momma and lies to tell each other. They never wasted a minute when it came to rewriting our family's story.

On the drive back, we dropped Bianca off first. Aunt Rita opened the door with her usual coldness, asked how the visit went, and disappeared inside before we could finish answering. Bianca didn't look back when she walked through the door. I stared at her until she vanished into the house, feeling a piece of me go with her.

I remembered that letter on the TV—the two-pager Rita wrote to Momma full of backhanded pity and outright betrayal. I couldn't believe it came from the same woman Momma once protected. I remembered when Rita's husband hit her. Momma didn't even hesitate. She loaded us up, grabbed Rita and her kids, and brought them home with us. No lectures, no guilt trips, just love. But people forget who saved them when it's no longer convenient to remember.

The rest of the ride, I kept my eyes on the window, watching the neighborhoods change as we headed back to Wendell's. Brick houses gave way to chain-linked fences, playgrounds turned to parking lots. I stayed quiet, trying to hold myself together.

When we finally got back, I grabbed Eric's bag and went straight to my room. I closed the door and locked it behind me. I didn't want anyone asking me how I felt, not that they would. I just needed space, to release everything I couldn't say.

The anger came fast. I paced the room, then sat on the bed, holding one of Momma's letters. I read it twice before placing it gently back in my box. My chest felt tight, like something pressed down on me. I lay on the bed, letting the tears fall where no one could see them. I cried until I fell asleep.

Later that week, I started writing again, letters to Momma filled with stories about Eric, about school, about the weather. I left out the parts that mattered most. I never told her about Bianca's growing silence or Eric calling Wendell "Momma" sometimes when he got confused. I didn't tell her how lonely I felt or how often I cried myself to sleep. I told her what Granny wanted me to say: only the good stuff.

I drew little cartoons in the corners like she used to. I copied lyrics from songs that made me think of her. I'd send her three or four letters a week, just to make sure her name was called at mail time. I pictured her sitting there with a bundle of letters in her lap, smiling at the silly doodles and carefully chosen words.

And sometimes, when I ran out of things to say, I just wrote, "I love you, Momma. I miss you every single day."

I still thought about Bianca constantly. We didn't see each other every weekend like we were supposed to. Sometimes, church was the only time. And church wasn't a place for playing or catching up. It was a place for pretending. Pretending we were okay. Pretending we were just regular kids with regular families.

But we weren't. We never would be.

Some days, I'd find myself staring at the front door, wondering what it would be like if Momma walked in. What if she came back early? What if the lawyers finally did what they promised? I'd imagine her scooping up Eric, holding Bianca tight, brushing my hair back and telling me I'd done good.

Even when the world felt like it was burning down around me, I held on to that image. That dream. That hope.

It was the only thing keeping me from falling apart completely.

LETTER FROM MOMMA

15 April 1997

Hello Jaydah,

I got your letters. I haven't written because my money didn't come. Tell your sister, Bianca, that I love and miss you all. I don't know what a private school costs, but you know I'll work hard at two jobs if that's what you want. I know you feel that school is hard right now and are concerned about scholarships, but your grades will improve. Just don't cheat your way through life. That's the reason I'm here. Don't concern yourself with material things. Eric's hair is nap, nap, nappy =) You are so crazy, I miss laughing with you, I can see your crazy smile. I enjoyed the song you wrote to me, as usual, you are the soul of my soul. Well, Granny is supposed to bring you down to see me. Let Aunt Wendell know to send that letter to my judge; they are trying to get me out of here. I'm sending you, your brother, and your sister all my love and kisses. Love you, soul of my soul.

Luv Momma

CHAPTER 22

Blood-stained Shorts

The smell of pancakes and syrup woke me up. It was Saturday, and Aunt Shay was in the kitchen, flipping pancakes like she was performing for an audience, her back turned but aware of everything happening around her. "Get dressed after breakfast," she said without turning around. "We're headed to Fish and Yella's game."

I rolled out of bed slowly, dragging my feet toward the bathroom. The shower was already running, and I let the water hit my skin longer than usual. The hot drops were the only warmth I allowed myself to feel in that house. I leaned against the wall, closing my eyes and pretending the water could wash away more than just dirt.

When I got out, I dried off quickly and threw on a pair of shorts and a loose t-shirt. It was already getting hot outside, and I didn't want to deal with heat and discomfort. I tied up my hair and met everyone by the front door. Eric was in his car seat, babbling to himself. Fish and Yella were fighting over who got to bring which ball. Wendell was rushing everyone, her keys already jingling in her hand. We loaded up the car and took off.

As we pulled out of the driveway, I found myself staring out of the window. My mind drifted. I imagined Momma standing in a field somewhere, wearing a soft blue sundress. Her arms were open, and her smile was full. I'd never seen her wear anything but a white jumpsuit in the past two years. But in my dream, she looked like herself again, free, beautiful, alive.

And then, just like that, the cramping started.

It crept in slow, then stronger. My stomach tightened, and a familiar nausea settled in. My period had started and I wasn't prepared. My heart sank.

"Wendell, can we stop at the store? I need to get some women's stuff," I asked, trying to keep my voice calm.

She didn't even glance back. "Why didn't you take care of all that before we left the house?"

"I didn't know it was gonna come today," I said quickly, already nervous.

"Well, girls supposed to know their body, Jaydah."

"Sorry, I didn't know. Can we please stop?" My voice cracked. "PLEASE?"

"You just gone have to wait and see if somebody got something when we get to the park," she said sharply.

I froze. I couldn't believe what I was hearing. Like I had control over this. Like I could tell my body to hold off just for today.

By the time we got to the park, it was too late. I could feel it. My shorts were damp. I sat still, my face burning with embarrassment and anger. Everyone got out of the car. Wendell was all smiles, calling out to other moms and waving to coaches. Shay followed behind her, holding baby Alex and looking cool and collected.

I stayed in the car, praying they wouldn't notice.

But they did.

They whispered. They looked. Shay walked back to the car and opened the door. "Come on, Jaydah."

"I can't," I whispered. "My period started. Wendell wouldn't stop for pads. I already leaked."

She sighed. "Ain't nothing wrong with that. Women have their periods. They understand."

I stared at her. "Would you walk around like this?" She didn't answer.

"If you want to stay in the car, then fine," Wendell chimed in from behind her. "We're here now. Make the best of it."

I couldn't believe how cruel they were. I shifted in the seat and saw the stain spreading on my shorts. I sat perfectly still, trying not to make it worse. A few moments later, Wendell returned with a towel.

"Get up," she said abruptly.

I hesitated.

"Now."

I stood, trembling, and she placed the towel down, then forced me to sit on top of it. I could see the disgust in her face. She walked off quickly, pretending like nothing was wrong.

I sat there for hours, shrinking further into myself. I kept my knees pulled tight to my chest. My stomach cramped hard, and the sun made it worse. I eventually dozed off, only to wake to Fish and Yella's laughter.

They climbed into the car, took one look at me, and both backed away.

"I ain't sitting next to her," Fish said.

"Eww, she bled all over the seat," Yella added.

I didn't even respond. I stared ahead and said nothing. The whole ride home was silent. My chest was tight, my throat dry. I could feel tears threatening, but I fought them off. They wouldn't get that from me. Not today.

When we pulled into the driveway, I waited for everyone to get out of the car first. Wendell didn't even look at me. I climbed out and walked toward the house, knowing everyone's eyes were on me. I felt like a walking scarlet letter.

In the house, I grabbed a clean pair of underwear and my towel. I locked the bathroom door behind me and stripped down. I balled up the stained shorts and stuffed them into the bottom of the trash can. I didn't want any reminders. I stood in the shower for a long time, letting the water burn. I bit down on a towel to muffle the sobs. They were loud this time. I didn't care.

Back in my room, I curled under my blanket and tried to disappear. My body ached. My heart ached worse. I wanted Momma so bad. I imagined her walking into the room, holding a heating pad and rubbing my back the way she used to. I could almost hear her voice, soft and low, "It's okay, baby."

But she wasn't there.

Later that night, I tried to write a letter to Momma. I started a few lines, then scratched them out. I wanted to tell her what happened, how Wendell humiliated me, but I knew it would only hurt her. And I couldn't do that.

I wanted to be strong.

As I laid in bed that night, wrapped in silence, I could feel the heat of the day still clinging to my skin. I kept thinking about how the blood dried into the seat and my clothes, how I sat out there exposed in more ways than one. I wondered if any of the women who had walked by had ever gone through the same thing, stuck, humiliated, wishing someone, anyone, would see them and say, "You don't deserve this." But nobody had. At least, that's what I thought until the next morning.

We were loading up again for another game, and I made sure I had plenty of pads with me. While unpacking the car at the park, Wendell walked off to drop off the chairs and cooler at the bleachers, leaving me alone by the car. I leaned against the car, arms crossed, stomach in knots. A woman I'd seen before, one of the other moms, was parked beside us. She glanced over, then stepped out of her car and walked toward me slowly.

"You alright, baby?" she asked gently.

I froze, unsure if I should answer. That wasn't a question I was routinely asked.

She leaned in, voice low. "I saw what happened yesterday.

That wasn't right."

My throat tightened.

"I keep some extra stuff in my car for my daughter," she continued, opening her trunk and pulling out a small zip pouch. "Here. Some pads, wipes if you need 'em. Ain't no shame in needing help."

I stared at her for a moment, too stunned to cry. I reached out and took the bag slowly, whispering, "Thank you."

"Being a young woman is hard enough without people trying to shame you for it," she said, giving me a little side hug before walking away. "Take care of yourself, okay?"

It was the first time in a long while I felt seen. Not pitied.

Not judged.

I sat down on the bleachers to watch the game without saying a word to Wendell or Shay. I promised myself one day, when I was older, I'd be that kind of woman for someone else.

Later that night, I found myself lying in bed again, this time with a different kind of ache - the ache of remembering better days. I turned onto my side and closed my eyes, letting the memory come like a film on a screen behind my eyelids.

My period was not regular, and I had my first one the summer before Momma left. We were in our old apartment. I remember waking up and feeling wet and panicked. I'd thought I'd peed myself. When I went to the bathroom and saw the blood, I called out for her, crying.

She came in, eyes wide but calm. "It's alright, baby," she said, kneeling beside me and brushing the hair out of my face. "You just started your period, that's all, nothing to be scared about."

She didn't yell. Didn't shame me. She ran a warm bath, sat on the edge, and showed me how to use a pad. "Every woman goes through it," she said, "but I'm proud you came to me."

After I was cleaned up, she put a warmed heating pad on my belly. We sat on the couch wrapped in a blanket, and she told me stories about her first time, how Granny had reacted, and the way no one really prepares you for how weird it feels.

"You don't ever have to feel embarrassed about being a woman," she said, "and don't let anybody ever make you feel dirty for it."

That memory brought warmth and sorrow I didn't know how to hold. My body missed her just as much as my heart did. And now, without her, something as natural as my period made me feel like I was disgusting.

That night, I didn't cry into my pillow like I usually did. I just stared at the ceiling, heart beating quietly, body still aching from the humiliation but mind a little clearer. That woman at the park reminded me I didn't have to believe the lies Wendell told me through her silence and neglect. I wasn't unworthy. I wasn't disgusting.

I was a girl becoming a woman without a mother to walk her through it, but not without strength.

The next time I got my period, I made sure I had what I needed. I packed my own bag with pads, wipes, and spare underwear. I made sure I'd never be caught that vulnerable again; if no one else would look out for me, I would.

I didn't tell Momma about the incident on our next visit, but I came close. When she cupped my chin and said, "I know, baby," I felt like she really did. Like somehow, she knew everything. I held her hand a little longer that day. Squeezed it like I didn't want to let go.

Because in all the blood, shame, silence, and cruelty, she was still the only one who made me feel clean.

LETTER FROM MOMMA

9 Jun 1997

Hello my Baby,

I got your letters. Thank you for sending the pictures; they looked pretty in those shorts. Baby, Momma is so sorry that I got myself into this mess and left you, but I pray to God that I'll be home soon. I know how you feel, but believe me, you belong to God and me. Right now, I'm not there to protect you from the hateful things Shay and Wendell say and do. I was mad when I read your letter. I wanted to curse them out, but, honey, the love of God made me realize we have to pray for them. The next time something happens, don't fuss with them; just tell them 'God bless you.' Baby, people who hurt others are often unhappy with themselves, but just be my big girl and pray about it. I really, really love you, so don't be sad because you can count on my love. I'm praying daily to get out of this place and get home to you. Keep being sweet; take care of my nappy-head Bianca and little man. Remember, no matter what, we are a family; you have a mother who loves you no matter what. You are the soul of my soul, heart of my life. Hugs and kiss noogies.

Love Mom

CHAPTER 23

A Young Woman

By my freshman year of high school, Momma had been gone three whole years. I finally gave up hope she would come and rescue me and focused on survival.

Wendell decided it would be easier for me to live with Granny than with her and Shay. Living with Granny gave me a little more freedom. Granny worked around the clock, and Dye worked nights. Uncle Junior was a crack head, so he never paid attention to anybody but the television. When he got his government check every first of the month, he was nowhere to be found. So, really, there was nobody but me.

I decided I would never tell a soul what I was going through. I wanted to be just like every other kid and didn't need anybody feeling sorry for me. I didn't need any handouts. I kept my life secrets to myself and finished out my whole freshman year without telling a soul of my mother's whereabouts.

Freshman year was very different than the others. It was the beginning of a new life, one without tears, hurt, or pain caused by the actions of Wendell and Shay. It was a life of freedom. For the first time since my momma left, I felt normal. I wasn't hounded every day about the wrong my mother did, the many reasons, lies, and tales of how she ended up where she is. My granny never spoke of it. In her mind, she felt her child was innocent and God was going to deliver her to us any day now.

I had made a lot of friends that year and was known as an untouchable, meaning I was hard to get, which made boys afraid even to tell me they were feeling me.

During my sophomore year, I got my first boyfriend. I was kind of happy about it. All my friends had begun dating and were experiencing the joys of puppy love. I hadn't given boys a thought the past few years because of the chaos with Momma but it finally felt good to be paired with the opposite sex. Louis McGee was tall, dark, and handsome, much different from me. He moved to Texas from Louisiana with his mom, brother, sister, and of course, the boyfriend.

His parents had gone through a long, hard divorce. Louis blamed himself for the breakup. He told me he was fucking with an older girl who lived next door. He would sneak her over, fuck her, and then she would leave. He told me one day he came home from school and found his door wide open, his momma and daddy screaming. Then, the girl ran past him with little to nothing on. The way he put it, that day was the end of his life and he vowed he would never look at his father the same. He said the bitch had the nerve to run past him and look him dead in his eye. He could tell from the look on her face she had no remorse. He carried some guilt about the situation and felt if had never brought her around, his daddy would have never slept with her.

They moved out that day and stayed with an aunt, then his mother met a new man and they moved to Texas. Louis and I were opposite, but it attracted me to him. He was rough and street-smart, accustomed to a hard life and found a way to get everything he wanted, no matter the cost. I was a little light-skinned red bone, as they say, standing about 5'2, and thick. I never noticed until that year how well I filled out. I was always self- conscious about my body because Carmen was much smaller, and Aunt Rita called me a fat ass one day when Carmen and I got into an argument. I was innocent. Wendell and Shay hid me from the world by dressing me in crazy dresses and keeping me in the house. Louis let me know how fine I was, though, and he acted as if he gave a damn about me. I didn't care too much about the whole boyfriend part of it; he made me feel like I was worth something, that I was beautiful and special.

My momma had told me all those things but in her absence, I doubted it. It was weird because nobody paid attention to me, not even Granny. I was sure if I disappeared, nobody would have noticed, but Louis fed my growing ego.

We dated the rest of the school year into the summer. I found myself walking almost an hour to see him, and he would do the same for me. He started to touch me in ways I had never been touched, the way Momma said no boy was supposed to touch me. We would go to the park, and he would put his hands in my pants and let his fingers go to work. One day, he told me he wanted to show me something. I met him in a secluded part of my apartment complex.

"Jaydah, don't be scared," he said.

"What are you about to do, Louis?" I replied.

He unbuttoned his khaki shorts and pulled it out. I was so mortified that I immediately turned around and ran all the way back home. I was disgusted and terrified. I had never seen a man's thang in real life. I heard a gentle knock at the door and when I looked out the window, it was Louis. I have slowly opened the door and stepped out.

"Jaydah, baby, I'm sorry I scared you," he said.

"I just feel like we are growing closer, and I wanted to show you what it looked like in person.

I know you're a virgin and never been with no one like you've been with me, and I love you. I wanted to share something special with you"

"Louis that thing doesn't look like the ones in the nasty movies"

"I'm not circumcised; that's why it looks so different."

My nerves started to settle a little. We began walking and talking.

"Have you ever had sex with a girl before?" I asked.

"I have, remembered the chick my daddy had sex with and one other girl.

Jaydah I don't want you to do anything you don't want to do, but we've been getting physical, and it might happen."

We talked about it a few times, kissed, and he would finger me. That whole experience was so new. I didn't know how to control it. By the end of the summer, I was no longer a virgin. I folded under pressure and wanted to get it over with anyway. I think half of me even wanted to do it to spite Momma for not being there - my first rebellious act. I didn't want to do it again after that; for me, it was just a one-time thing, plus I feared Momma would be ashamed of me. He accepted my decision, so he said. I had no good or bad feelings about it; I didn't feel anything.

Sophomore year, everybody had their eyes on me and Louis because we had been together for 8 months, a long time for teenagers. I could see the females' faces frowning and wondering when they could have their turn with him, and the dudes checking me out, waiting for Louis to slip up. Louis wasn't studying none of them bitches though.

One day, we decided to skip school and go to Louis' crib. He had a homeboy, Kasey, who had a girlfriend named Toya. Everything was cool when we first arrived; we were chilling while Louis and

Kasey puffed on a blunt. Toya and I sat outside on the porch. The boys walked outside to join us and Kasey started kissing and licking Toya's neck. He started grabbing at her and squeezing her breast and booty. I could tell by her moans that she was into it. Louis began to kiss me. I pulled away and looked him in the eyes, hoping he would see what I was thinking and feeling. Kasey led Toya through the front door and into Louis' room. Louis looked at me and said,

"It's okay, I know you don't want to do it."

Damn right, I thought to myself while smirking at him.

"I just want to lay on the bed and kiss. They're gonna do it, but we don't have to," he assured.

We climbed into his bed and a thousand thoughts ran through my head while Kasey and Toya were already in the full act on the bunk bed across the room.

He was rough, not soft and gentle as he had been the first time. He kissed me hard, grabbed at my breasts and body.

I whispered to him, "Stop, I don't want to have sex."

He looked at me with a strange look as if he was telling me to just go with the flow.

"Only kissing," I said to him.

He shook his head and unbuttoned my pants. I was so speechless, I didn't know what to say. My body froze up, and I couldn't get my thoughts together. All I could say was stop. I heard myself repeat the word over and over again, but it didn't mean shit to him because he was undressing himself from the waist down. I started to push at him, and he grabbed my hands. I could feel the tears rolling down my cheeks and heard my own nose sniffling, but he kept going. I covered my face and cried until he was done. He rolled over and kissed me.

"I'm sorry. I just couldn't look bad in front of my boy."

I could already hear Kasey and Toya in the shower, playing around. When they were done, I asked to take my shower alone. I ran the bath water as hot as I could and washed as hard as I could, but no matter how much soap I used, I still felt so dirty. I went home right after and fell asleep.

Wendell came and picked me up for lunch the next day because I had a dentist appointment. She asked if living with Granny was something I wanted to continue to do.

Hell yeah, I thought. She started talking to me about boys and sex, and all I could do was lower my head.

She said, "If you need anything, let me know, Jaydah. It's a lot of STDs floating around out there and you need to protect yourself if you are doing anything. If you're having sex, you need to tell me so I can get you checked out."

I was so scared. I didn't want to tell her, I thought she would be mad. I wasn't planning on doing it again, so why tell?

"You can trust me, I won't tell, but if you're doing anything, then you gotta let me know 'cause there could be something wrong and you can't see it."

She was right. If there was something wrong, I wouldn't know unless I got checked out. Hell, Louis wasn't a virgin, he had been fucking. So, I gathered up enough courage and told her. She looked at me, relieved, and said she would schedule an appointment for me soon. After that, I felt like I could tell her everything, that maybe she wasn't as bad as she appeared to be. I felt like for the first time, somebody besides Louis—even though he did what he did—cared. When I went home that day, I did my homework and relaxed. Louis called, but I avoided his call. He knew why. I fell asleep thinking about Momma and how she would feel if she found out I wasn't innocent anymore. I wondered if she would still love me the same or think of me differently. She always said when I lost my innocence I wouldn't be her baby anymore, I'd be a woman.

I woke up to the silhouette of a short woman in the doorway. I heard her voice but couldn't understand what she was saying. Then, it was clear that it was Granny, and she was screaming and yelling about me losing my virginity. She was calling me every name but the child of God, and she walked up on me. I put my arm over my head in fear that she would hit me, but she didn't; she just got really close and screamed louder. She turned around and walked out, slamming the door behind her. I collapsed to the ground in disbelief Wendell broke her promise.

I was falling in and out of sleep when the phone rang. It was Wendell on the other line, apologizing for telling Granny about my secret. I felt sick to my stomach and blocked out the sound of her voice. I hung up the phone and forced myself to go back to sleep. I knew Granny wasn't the only one she told and in thirty minutes the whole family would know and I'd be labelled a whore by them too.

The next day at school, Louis was trying to be as sweet and sincere as possible. He bought me my favorite candy and paid for my lunch.

"Louis, we need to talk. What happened the other day wasn't cool and I can't get it off my mind," I explained to him.

He dropped his head and said he had something else to tell me. He looked me in the eyes and asked if I remembered a girl named Shondra.

"Yeah, I remember her."

"Well, the other day we were all swimming at the pool and I ended up fingering her," he confessed.

He dropped his head to the ground again and whimpered a little. For some reason, I wasn't mad, but relieved - relieved I had a good enough reason to let him go. After what he did to me that day, the sight of him disgusted me anyway, and I knew I couldn't avoid him anymore. I told him it was okay, and maybe we shouldn't be together.

I turned to walk away, and he grabbed my hand.

"No matter what, I'll always love you," he said, his eyes watering.

I glanced at him and walked away. That was the last time I ever talked to him. I saw him around school with several other girls but I never spoke to him again.

It had been a couple of months since we visited Momma, and of course, Granny wanted to go right after I lost my virginity.

"Get up, it's time to go." Granny came in yelling,

The bed felt so good when I tried to get up; it felt like the pillows wrapped themselves around me and pulled back. I wanted to look nice for Momma, so I showered thoroughly, dressed nicely, and put on a little makeup so she could see how much of a little lady I had become.

We got in the car and were on our way to get Eric and Bianca. We pulled up to Aunt Rita's house, and I could see Bianca staring out the window with a big kiddie smile. Granny opened the door and had a disappointed look on her face. Bianca was wearing some tacky, old outfit, and her hair was all over her head. It seemed Aunt Rita had just let her dress herself and hadn't even tried to assist.

Granny was mad.

"Jaydah, go find ya sista something to wear to see ya momma!" she shouted, making sure that Rita heard.

"Damn shame, letting that baby go see her momma in prison looking like that," she mumbled.

Granny was steaming hot. I grabbed Bianca and led her to the room to change.

Rita made it clear to Bianca when she first moved in she wasn't babysitting and that Bianca would have to learn to care for herself and contribute. I always wondered why someone would take in kids they didn't want to help. Momma had been gone for four years. The whole four years, all we heard was how lucky we were they took us in, put a roof over our heads and food in our mouths. I was thankful for their kindness and still hoped someday I would feel loved. I knew they weren't my mother, but I thought family was still supposed to love you no matter what. They drilled how we shouldn't complain about being separated and the word 'Momma' was not a weapon we could use to comfort ourselves or say to help when being verbally attacked. The sound of the word was even stranger to say. It was like a two-year-old saying bitch.

By the time I finished dressing Bianca, Wendell had arrived with Eric. I could tell by Granny's silence that she was agitated. Her daughters were making the trip difficult for her, and none of them offered her any support. That day, I realized just how hard it was on her as she limped to the car. I never noticed that limp before that day, but I could see it was painful. When we got in the car, she rubbed her knees, closed her eyes, and let out a long sigh. I could see her thin, small lips part to release the air, as if all the trouble that knee was causing her came out through them. She lowered her head, smiled, and said, "Let's hit the road, Jacks." Granny made small talk and asked Bianca how she was doing, and I slept the whole way there.

When I woke, we pulled up to the barbed wire gate. I unloaded Bianca and carried Eric in my arms while Granny pulled herself out of the car, taking breaks in between to rest her aching knee. She limped to the gate, shaking her head, and pressed the buzzer. "How may I help you?" said a voice.

"We are here to see inmate number 758911." "Step back."

A little petite police officer came to the gate and asked for all IDs. She looked at me.

"This is her daughter; she is still a minor," Granny said.

"How old is she?"

"She is only fourteen," she lied.

"Well, I'll let ya'll in, but she needs to get an ID at fifteen."

She opened that gate and let us through. I felt relieved. I thought I wasn't going to be able to see my momma. We sat inside for the first time. It was weird; we weren't used to being in such close proximity to the other inmates.

Momma came through the door, and I saw a big smile on her face. Granny gave us one last warning before she approached.

Momma walked up and gave us a hug and kisses. Bianca hugged Momma's thigh and Eric joined in. Guess him seeing Bianca do it made him feel comfortable embracing Momma.

"Hello, my lady Jaydah. How are you?"

I smiled, hugged, and kissed her, making sure Eric was in between us, hoping to transfer the comfort I felt with Momma to him. She kissed us both, and he didn't pull away or fight it.

Granny couldn't wait to put me on front street. She immediately blurted out, "Jaydah got something to tell you." Momma looked over at me, and I dropped my head. I knew what Granny was referring to and I was so angry she brought it up that way. Momma rubbed my back.

"What is it, Jaydah?"

"Well, momma, I ..."

"She had sexual intercourse for the first time," Granny interrupted.

My face felt hot, and I couldn't believe she'd done that to me. It was my mistake, and I should have been able to tell my mother anyway I pleased, especially after not seeing her for the past few months. I felt robbed of the right to have a conversation with my own mother. I hated feeling like I was under the microscope every time I wanted to tell her something. Momma held my chin in her hand, kissed me, and said, "Jaydah, no need to be ashamed, we all have done it. Now you're a woman."

I hated those words. I enjoyed and took comfort in the thought of being my mommy's baby girl, even though I was fifteen years old. She rubbed my back, said, "Everything's gonna be alright," and winked at me.

She whispered, "We'll talk later."

Momma quickly changed the subject and began to tell us about how one of her roommates tried to steal from her. Momma always said she hated a liar and a thief more than anything. It sounded like one of those movies on Lifetime. She mentioned one inmate attempted to steal a box of Debbie Snacks from her.

"Momma, tell us what happened, and don't leave nothing out," I said with excitement.

"Well, it was lights out, right? I had just got out the beauty shop and was taking my shower. When I got out, I went to my area and lay on the bed to go to sleep. I rolled over and wanted a snack and noticed the whole damn box of Swiss Cake Rolls was gone. You know I was pissed."

"What happened next, Momma, how you find out who took 'em?"

"Well, it was only one other girl up that night, and when I noticed they were gone, I saw her ass tryna fake like she was sleep. I didn't say anything, I decided I was just going to wait until the next day to see if she was going to come clean, right, and give me my stuff. So, I waited until lights out, looked over the wall at her bed, and said, "Phillips, if you took my cakes let me know now. I'm not playing, my seventy two year old momma work hard to put money on my books so I can buy what I want and what I need." She just looked at me and I nodded my head."

Momma told how she hemmed her up in the bathroom and whooped her ass. Then, went through her stuff and found her Debbie snacks. She said that girl didn't touch any of her stuff from then on, and she even offered her some after that, but she was too scared even to say yes. I laughed inside, thinking to myself, *That's my momma.*

Granny enjoyed hearing the stories, too, but she didn't want us glorifying prison life. She didn't want us to think that prison was okay. Even my aunts tried to get together and make the decision my brother and sister were too young to feel comfortable about visiting the prison. Hell, that's where my momma was and if any one of them was locked up, they would want to see their kids, too. That visit turned out to be a good one.

While kissing Momma goodbye and walking away from her, I noticed Granny's knee was feeling better, or at least that was how it appeared. Granny got her ID and as soon as we walked out of the security gates, she started to limp again. She knew Momma would look down the hill sometimes and watch us load up the car and drive off, so she played it smooth until she felt outta sight.

On the way back, we stopped in West Texas to get something to eat. Then, we were back on the road again. By the time we made it back home, everyone in the car was asleep except for Granny.

We dropped off Bianca and I could tell by the strength in her hug she did not want to let go. Sadness filled my heart. Every time we visited Momma, it was like we had our life back; when we left, it felt like we lived that day she went to prison and never came home over and over again. I didn't cry, though, and neither did

Bianca. Living with Rita in a house full of kids gave her the strength she needed to cope with the life she was forced to live.

We pulled off, and I could see Bianca's small hands in the window waving goodbye, then the little fingers disappeared behind the curtain. We pulled up to Wendell's to drop off Eric, and as soon as we pulled up, Wendell was waiting. Wendell grabbed Eric, and Fish came running outside in his underwear, kissing Eric. I could hear Wendell say, "You miss Momma? Momma missed you, poo poo head." I rolled my eyes in disgust and walked Eric's car seat into the house. I was happy Granny was in a hurry because I couldn't wait to get away from there.

The ride home was quiet. I could tell Granny had a lot on her mind. When we got home, she ran herself a bath. I could hear her moan in pain as she got up from the tub and limped her way into her bedroom. Sometimes, I would go and massage her legs for her with some mint-smelling lotion and then fall asleep with her.

Granny was very bold and knew how to embarrass you, but she was the most understanding person I had ever known. She had compassion, too, and tried never to judge. If someone we knew didn't have a home and were going through a tough time, Granny would take them in without question. She wouldn't ask for anything in return; they could stay for however long it took them to get back on their feet again. She was a good woman, just explosive if you pushed her to the limit.

LETTER FROM MOMMA

21 July 1997

Hello Jaydah,

Mommie loves you. I wish I were there to tell you every day that you are special and that I love you. I haven't written because I didn't have any stamps or money to buy any, sorry. But don't worry, honey, mother will always love you. When you start feeling sad, think in your mind and know in your heart that you have a mother who loves you till the day she dies. I miss you so much, my sweet daughter. Sometimes, I cry myself to sleep at night, too. It doesn't matter where we live when I come home, as long as we're together. I don't know when I'll be home, but stay sweet and strong for me. I know that sometimes you get mad and sometimes you're sad, but that's okay. I get mad, too, because I want to leave here and go home. Mad because I'm here and not there to hold you and tell you I love you, because I let myself get into this mess, and now I can't be home with my little children. I know that it's all for a reason. Tell Bianca I will write her this week. Jaydah, thanks for the love you send. I love you so much. Mommie will be home soon.

Luv always Mommie

Soul of my Soul

PART IV

WHAT I CARRIED IN SILENCE

Growing Without Guidance

CHAPTER 24

Pretty Hurts

For a long time, Carmen and I had been like sisters more than cousins—raised under roofs that echoed the same laughter, got the same whoopings, shared the same secrets. But somewhere along the way, things shifted. I couldn't pinpoint exactly when, but I felt it in the air, in the stares, in the backhanded compliments that started coming from her more and more often.

It wasn't just the usual growing pains. It was something sharper, something heavy that hung in the space between us. Maybe it started when I moved in with Granny and Aunt Dye—far away from the chaos of bouncing house to house. Carmen lived with her mother, who was strict and perfection-obsessed. Their household was polished on the outside, but tense on the inside, where everyone smiled with their teeth but squinted with their eyes.

Meanwhile, my life was loud and complicated but full of little freedoms. I was surviving, yes, but I was also figuring out how to live.

We were only about a year and a half apart, Carmen thirteen going on thirty, and me at fifteen. I was juggling school, the majorette team, and a rotating door of side hustles: doing hair in the back room of Nanny's house, letting my godsisters steal clothes for me from the mall, and getting a crisp twenty dollars a month from Wendell when she was in a good mood. Miss Angie, my best friend's mom, also helped out, handing me little extras here and there without making a fuss.

Carmen didn't have to hustle like that. Her mom bought her things. Clean, pastel-colored church suits with matching kitten heels and lip gloss from Bath & Body Works. Carmen used them like magic, especially around Antwan.

Now, Antwan. He was seventeen and fine in that quiet, respectful way that made you wonder what he was thinking. Light brown skin, tight curls, almond-shaped eyes, and the cleanest white smile you ever saw. He lived in a nice neighborhood, with a two-parent home, drove his own car. He even smelled like something royal. He was smart, nerdy, but charming once he warmed up – the kind of boy you wanted to sit next to at church just to see if he'd glance your way during the sermon.

Carmen had been eyeing him for a while. She would giggle when he walked in, make sure her lip gloss shimmered under the sanctuary lights, and drop little comments like, "I think Antwan looked at me today." I wasn't paying much attention to him at first. I had way too much going on to be worried about some boy. But things took a turn when Carmen invited me to the movies with her one weekend, saying it'd be the first time we could go without any adults tagging along.

What she didn't tell me was that Antwan would be meeting us there. As soon as we walked inside, I saw him strolling toward us with that shy smile, and everything clicked. This was a setup. I was the third wheel. I pulled her aside and told her straight up she was too young to be talking to Antwan. She gave me that eyeroll and said, "I'm about to be fourteen in a few weeks. Girl, it isn't even that serious."

Antwan sat between us during the movie, but his body leaned toward me the whole time. His questions and his jokes were directed toward me. He gave Carmen the big brother energy, while he gave me something else. After the movie, he asked for my number, casually, as if he were asking for gum. He told Carmen we were all friends but it didn't take long before the calls became just him and me.

That was the beginning of the end.

Carmen swore she didn't care. Claimed she was already talking to another boy. But the vibe changed. Her giggles turned into eyerolls. Her friendliness started to curdle. And then the comments came.

"She's doing too much."

"She always gotta be seen."

"She really thinks she cute."

I tried to ignore it, but it got harder when she started teaming up with her mom. Suddenly, I was being compared to Carmen more than ever. "You should carry yourself more like Carmen." "Carmen doesn't need all that attention." "Why don't you act more like her?" Even Bianca started to feel it. They'd throw slick comments her way too, and we'd just look at each other like, "Here we go again." We'd grown used to it, trading whispered affirmations back and forth, building each other up in a house where we were rarely poured into.

Then came summer vacation.

Dee had decided to take Bianca and me to Cali for a visit. He felt Eric was too young to bring along, so he left him with Aunt Wendell. We spent a full week away, just the three of us. He treated us like royalty. Bought us new clothes, spoiled us with love, and took us to a salon where I got my hair dyed honey blonde. Not just any blonde. It was soft, warm, and made my straightened coils look like they'd been kissed by sunlight. For the first time, I felt radiant. Like all the versions of myself I had kept hidden were now shining through.

When I got back, church was the first stop. I walked through those double doors with my new hair flowing down my back, a fresh outfit on, fitted, but not disrespectful, and confidence in my step. The second I entered; I caught Antwan's eyes. He dropped his head and smiled like, "That's all me." That silent, satisfied grin said everything.

I slid into the pew next to Bianca, and we both noticed Carmen whispering to Chad, her eyes darting toward me. I leaned in just close enough to hear: "Her clothes are so inappropriate for church."

The sting was immediate. She said it like I was a stranger, not the same girl with whom I used to sneak snacks in Grandma's kitchen or cry from laughing too hard during sleepovers. Her voice had that sharp tone, soaked in jealousy, and for the first time, I really saw her. Not as my cousin. Not as my sister-friend. But as a rival.

The jealousy had rooted deep. I was the girl Antwan called now. The one he wrote late-night texts to. The one he picked up in that clean white car. He was proud of me, not just because of how I looked, but because of how I carried myself. I still made the honor roll. I still led the majorette team. I was building something with the few tools I had, love, hustle, and an unshakable belief my story wasn't finished.

Carmen couldn't see that. She only saw what she thought I had taken from her. But I wasn't trying to compete. I was just trying to survive.

And honestly? Pretty did hurt.

It hurt to be the one who didn't grow up in the safe house. Who didn't have the new clothes bought straight from the store, who had to do her own hair in the mirror while balancing a baby brother on her hip. It hurt to be seen and then punished for being seen. To be admired by strangers but critiqued by family.

But still, I walked in beauty. I walked in grit.

Antwan and I had our own moments. Our own laughter. Like the time he took me to a secret car rally, and the police showed up. He told me to jump in, and I did, half laughing, half screaming, as we sped off down the street, tires burning. The adrenaline, the thrill, the way we pulled into his driveway gasping and breathless, it felt like something out of a movie.

He never tried me. Never pushed past boundaries. He just liked to be near me. I liked being seen by someone who saw more than just my hips and hair. He saw my fire. My hurt. My hustle.

Meanwhile, Carmen drifted, more snide comments, more silence.

I could've gone petty. I could've clapped back. But I didn't. I held my head high and poured more love into Bianca and Eric. I focused on school. I worked my little jobs and braided hair 'til my fingers cramped. I dreamed about Momma, read every word of her letters, and prayed she'd come home soon. I missed her so much it burned sometimes.

But I was okay. More than okay. I was blooming in the cracks.

And Carmen?

Well, Carmen would have to deal with her own pretty hurting. Just like I did.

LETTER FROM MOMMA

24 September 1997

Jaydah,

Guess What? I love you, my sweet daughter. You say I'm not there to tell you I love you. Well, here's something I want you to remember: my love for you, my child, is 70 x 7 million x 7 trillion x forever. So, every day, take a little of that and remember you are always on my mind, in my heart, and in my prayers.

Love Momma,
Soul of my Soul

CHAPTER 25

Secrets and Sleepovers

Antwan's prom was just around the corner, and despite everything else going on in my life, I managed to save enough money for a gown that shimmered like it cost far more than it did. It was a deep crimson, meant to match his sharp red suit, and when I put it on in front of the mirror, I saw something I wasn't used to seeing: elegance, confidence, beauty that didn't ask permission to shine. For one night, I would not be the girl with the incarcerated mother or the girl hustling to make ends meet. I'd just be Jaydah, radiant and whole, on the arm of the boy who made me forget, even for a moment, that life had been anything but easy.

We took pictures on Granny's porch, the wooden railing barely holding steady as cousins leaned over to snap photos from every angle. I could feel everyone watching me, whispering about the hair, the dress, the boy. But I blocked them out. Antwan's hand on my waist grounded me. His "Damn you fine" whispered in my ear wrapped around me like a shield.

We danced slowly that night, under a ceiling of glittering lights in the high school gym. I let myself laugh, let myself feel soft. I even let myself imagine the future for a moment, a dorm room with pictures of us taped to the wall, a life where I didn't have to look over my shoulder or dodge questions about my momma. I hadn't done that in a long time. But when I did, it felt like a breath I didn't know I'd been holding.

By then, Antwan and I had mastered the art of sneaking around. Our "sleepovers" were never full nights, but slivers of closeness tucked between curfews and dawn. Sometimes I'd sneak in late and leave before anyone woke up. Other nights, we'd hide in each other's closets until the house was quiet and still, slipping out to whisper secrets and share sleepy kisses under the hush of midnight. Those moments were our rebellion, our claim to something sweet and secret in a world that had shown me more bitterness than tenderness.

Antwan was one of the few people I didn't have to lie to about my mother. He never asked me to explain the silence in her absence or press me for details. He just let it be. That quiet acceptance was more of a comfort than any sermon or forced prayer circle ever could be. My uncle and aunt, the pastor and first lady, made it a regular ritual at church to "pray over my burden," peeling back the scab every time like I wasn't standing right there, trying to hold it all together. Their prayers felt more like public announcements: a reminder I was the girl with a mother behind bars, the family's charity case wrapped in Sunday clothes.

But Antwan never once made me feel less than.

Still, keeping that truth tucked away at school was a full-time job. I lived in two worlds: one where I was surviving on grit and grace, and one where I had to pretend I had it all under control. It all came crashing down the day my majorette coach pulled me aside after practice. She had just posted the list for the national competition, including airline tickets, new uniforms, hotel fees, and meals. My name was right there near the top.

"I want you on this team, Jaydah," she said, eyes bright.

"You earned it."

I nodded slowly, holding the paper in my hands, trying not to let her see the panic rising in my chest.

"But," she continued, "you'll need to talk to your parents about covering the travel costs."

That was the moment I felt my throat close. There were no parents to call. No two-income household to back me. I tried to hold the tears in, but I couldn't. I broke down right there, in the middle of the gym, the words tumbling out like shame in fast forward.

"I can't afford it," I whispered. "I don't have parents. My mom's in prison. I've been paying for my own stuff; I just can't swing it this time."

Her face crumbled. She reached for me, tears welling up in her eyes too. She offered to pay for it all. Everything. Every single dollar.

I couldn't let her do that.

I wasn't a charity case. I clawed my way through life with pride, and even though I was tired, bone-deep tired, I wasn't going to let my dignity slip, not now. I thanked her and declined. After that day, I noticed my debt quietly disappeared. My uniforms were suddenly "extra" ones from storage. My dance fees were somehow "already covered." She never brought it up again. She just kept looking out for me in silence. And I loved her for that.

One night, Antwan and I sat in his car after practice, the parking lot mostly empty, our bags tossed into the backseat. We talked about nothing, songs we liked, what we'd do if we could skip town, and the best gas station snacks. I watched his fingers on the steering wheel, long and sure, and wondered how something so small, just being near him, could make me feel full.

"You ever think about running away?" I asked, not really joking.

He looked at me sideways. "All the time."

I exhaled and leaned back, my head hitting the headrest.

"Sometimes I feel like I'm living three lives. The girl everyone thinks I am, the girl I have to be, and the one I really am when no one's looking."

He reached over and touched my knee gently. "I see all three."

That was the thing about Antwan. He didn't say much, but when he did, it cut deep and clean.

Although Antwan and I were getting along well, I noticed a gradual change in him. He had started hanging out with a new crowd, older friends, cooler parties, and a girl. A pretty girl. She was loud spoken, with long box braids and wide eyes that batted too often when he was around. He said they were just friends, but I wasn't blind. I'd learned to see the signs before people said a word.

When we went to the prom, we danced and we smiled for pictures, but something was off. His hand didn't linger on my waist the way it used to.

By midsummer, we were drifting. Chad, my cousin now living with us, pulled me aside one day.

"He's with that girl now," he said flatly. "Been seeing her for a few weeks."

I didn't cry. I didn't yell. I just nodded. My heart had learned not to break so easily. I was too used to loss. I let Antwan go in silence, figuring that was the end of it.

Until he showed up on Granny's porch one humid afternoon.

Chad let him in, reluctantly. I was in the kitchen when I heard the knock, and when I turned the corner, there he was, hands in his pockets, eyes pleading.

"I messed up," he said. "I miss you."

I didn't respond. I just stood there, arms crossed, heart folding in on itself.

He took a step closer. "You're the one I love, Jaydah. I was just stupid."

I didn't stop him when he leaned in. Our lips met, and the fire between us reignited. We moved like we were starving for each other, like nothing had ever come between us. For a moment, it felt like old times, like we were whole again.

Afterwards, he smiled and whispered, "It's different with you. I'm happy we're back together."

I pulled back, looked him in the eyes, and said, "Back together?"

He blinked, confused.

"We're not back together," I said. "That was goodbye."

The look on his face was all the closure I needed. I walked him to the door and closed it behind him, sealing a chapter for good.

After that, I threw myself into school and dance. I dated here and there but nobody felt like Antwan. Still, I didn't have the luxury of holding on to heartbreak. I had siblings to protect. Dreams to chase. Letters from Momma to read late into the night when the world felt heavy. They didn't come as often anymore, but when they did, I read them like scripture. She was still my anchor, even behind bars.

I started journaling again. Not the neat kind with bullet points and goals. The messy, pages-ripped-from-the-spine kind. The kind of journaling where the pen feels like a shovel, digging up everything I tried to bury. My entries were full of half-truths and whispered prayers. Sometimes I wrote letters to Momma that I never sent. Sometimes I wrote to myself as if I were someone worth comforting.

Dear Diary,

I want someone to love all of me, not just the part that smiles in pictures. The part that gets tired, that misses her momma so bad it hurts in her chest? She's worthy too. I don't want to keep living in pieces.

It became a ritual. After everyone went to bed, I'd slip outside onto the porch with my notebook, sit beneath the dim porch light, and write until the crickets lulled me to sleep. Those nights were my real sleepovers, with my feelings, with my truth.

Junior year was coming to an end, and everything felt on the brink of changing. Even Bianca noticed. One afternoon, she peeked into my room while I was writing and sat on the edge of my bed, swinging her legs.

"You still talk to Antwan?" she asked, her voice soft, careful.

I shook my head. "Not like that. He's not my forever." She paused, then nodded. "Good. You deserve better." I looked up, surprised at how steady she sounded. "Since when you get so wise?" I teased. She smiled. "Since watching you."

That hit me harder than any heartbreak. Because all this time, I thought I was hiding the hard stuff, the loneliness, the loss. But she saw it. And somehow, my surviving had become her strength too.

As the summer heat intensified and the school year drew to a close, I decided I was done chasing approval. From boys. From family. From anyone who couldn't love the whole of me.

When the majorette coach nominated me to lead the summer youth camp for incoming freshmen, I said yes. I showed up every day in the blazing sun, teaching little girls how to hold their heads high while spinning batons and kicking in sync. It wasn't about the moves. It was about confidence. Command. Believing you deserved to take up space.

One day, one of the younger girls asked me, "Do you live with your mom?"

I froze for a second, then smiled and said, "No, but she's always with me."

I didn't explain. I didn't shrink. And it felt like reclaiming something sacred.

That August, on the eve of my senior year, I got a letter from Momma. Her handwriting was shakier than usual, but the words were strong:

My baby girl, I don't know how long I got left in here. But I need you to keep living. Not just surviving, but really living. Don't let what happened to me become what defines you. You're too full of light. I see you shining all the way from here.

I cried harder than I had in months. And for the first time, Bianca held me instead of me consoling her. We sat on the floor, both of us cross-legged and weepy, rereading the letter again and again.

Secrets and sleepovers had taught me about love and loss. About how sometimes the people you love will fail you. And sometimes the ones you least expect will save you.

I still dreamed of sleepovers, ones with my own kids someday, under covers with flashlights, laughing at nothing. Sleepovers where nobody had to sneak in or sneak out. Just joy and warmth and the sound of someone breathing beside you who really sees you.

But for now, I had myself. And that was enough.

Loving myself in pieces was the first step toward loving myself whole.

LETTER FROM MOMMA

1 October 1997

Hey Jaydah,

My precious girl, sorry I haven't written to you. I've been a little sad because I haven't seen you all in two months. I know school has started back. Thank you for your sweet letters. Yes, I think I'll be home for Christmas, keep praying. No, you guys can't cut Eric's hair, grease it, and brush it into two braids. Don't be letting him call everybody momma, either. I know he is a trip, too. Anyway, call Bianca, I'll be writing her, too. I'm thinking of you as always. Kiss everyone's nappy head for me, ok.

Love and kisses
Mommie

CHAPTER 26

On the Edge of Enough

There comes a moment when even the strongest shoulders sag under the weight of it all. For me, that moment came slowly, like a quiet unraveling, a single thread pulled too tight, stretching until it snapped. I had been holding it together for too long. For Momma. For Bianca and Eric. For everyone who expected me to keep rising, as if nothing had ever broken me. But something inside me was crumbling. And I didn't know how to stop it.

Since Momma went away, I had become a protector, a nurturer, a buffer, and a secret-keeper. But I hadn't had time to be a girl, a daughter, or a teenager just trying to figure herself out.

I was living with my cousin Chad, Aunt Dye, Granny, and Uncle Junior in a house with more chaos than comfort. Granny worked constantly, days, nights, doubles when she could get them. She was a good woman, no doubt, but we barely saw her. Aunt Dye was a night-shift LVN who stayed doped up on prescription pills half the time. And Uncle Junior? He was a high-functioning crackhead who managed to be funny as hell when he wasn't knee-deep in a binge.

Junior had this ability to live halfway normal for weeks, then disappear into a blur of smoke and paranoia, but he was respectful in his own way. If he asked to borrow money, he actually repaid it.

Sometimes I'd wait until he was posted up on the couch, high but chill, flipping through channels, then sneak down and hit the fuse box.

"Jaydaaah!" he'd holler, flailing around in the dark. "I'll skin you alive, little girl!"

I'd be up the stairs cackling. It was our twisted little game. Like we had an unspoken agreement to laugh when we could because there wasn't much else to do.

One day I said, "Uncle Junior, you homeless for real."

He looked me dead in the face and said, "Well, we homeless together, baby girl."

It stuck with me.

Because he was right. This whole time I thought I had a home just because I had a roof. But nobody asked me how school was. Nobody showed up to a single majorette performance. Nobody noticed when I stayed out all night. I was homeless in every way that mattered. Just another girl slipping through the cracks while people stepped over me like I was part of the floor.

Chad? He was the prince of the house. Got whatever he needed—rides, money, attention. His laugh could light up a room and the grown folks loved to brag on him. I watched it happen over and over. Favoritism wrapped in casual cruelty. The boys were given room to dream, to fail, to just be. The girls were given lists of things not to do, voices full of suspicion, and warnings about becoming "just like your momma."

The judgment was thick. My aunties never said it outright, but they didn't need to. I saw it in their eyes every time they looked at me. Like I was the walking embodiment of my mother's mistakes. Carmen, once my best friend, now whispered like she'd caught something from her mama's bitterness. "She just like her momma," I heard her say one day. "She gon' be pregnant before she's eighteen." It wasn't said to my face, but whispers grow teeth when they echo long enough.

It hurt because I wasn't out here wildin'. I wasn't sneaking around with random boys. I was dancing my heart out at practice, keeping my grades up, doing what I had to do. But nobody cared about the holding together part. They only noticed when something slipped.

And then came Jazz.

Jazz was the kind of girl who wore her trauma like lip gloss: shiny, loud, impossible to miss. She lived right next door to me. We weren't friends, but we'd known each other long enough to smile in passing. Until one day, she just stopped smiling.

I don't know what flipped the switch, but I figured it had something to do with how the boys treated me. They joked about her, not with her; they flirted disrespectfully and talked about her behind her back. With me, they laughed, looked out for me, and sat on the porch beside me without pushing up on me or disrespectfully talking to me. They called me "Lil Mama," and it felt like a badge of honor, not a setup. Jazz didn't understand that. All she saw was the respect I carried without even trying. It made her angry, and that anger turned into envy.

She started with little things, talking about me negatively all loud in the hallways at school, brushing past me harder than she had to, calling me "uppity" or saying "she think she too good." Then came the lies. She told people I slept with every boy on the block. Said I had diseases. She painted me out to be the very thing she was known for, hoping it would knock me off whatever pedestal she imagined I was on. Everybody knew that she had given her ex-boyfriend gonorrhea and talked about how she had a sour fishy smell. One boy even said he had seen green discharge when they were about to have sex once and was happy he didn't go through with it.

Then one night, my house got egged.

I didn't even need to go outside to know who it was, but I did, and when I saw the yolk dripping down the front door like the house was crying, something broke in me. I stood in the doorway, fists balled, breath caught, feeling like I had been peeled open in front of the whole world.

She lived right next door. That was the part that stung. She could walk back into the comfort of her mother's house like she hadn't just shattered the last piece of peace I had left. I lived there for years, and no one really knew until Chad moved in and started hanging with everyone. I was the girl you saw at school with no idea she lived next door—but not anymore, thanks to Chad. Now, all my admirers from school had access to me outside of school and Jazz was not happy about it.

I didn't confront her. I wanted to. But Momma raised me with a kind of pride that didn't let me act a fool in public. Aunt Dye came outside and cleaned up the mess, never mentioning the incident to Jazz or her mother. She didn't ask me why either, just brushed it off like it never happened. The messy yolk was washed away by evening.

But the mess inside me? That didn't wash off.

I pulled back from everything after that. Some of the students believed Jazz's lies. Most of them knew the truth, but it still made me feel some type of way.

Coach pulled me aside one day. Said I looked different. I had dropped a significant amount of weight.

"Are you eating? Everything alright at home?" I smiled. Lied. Said I was just tired.

She put her hand on my shoulder. "You don't have to be strong all the time, Jaydah. You're allowed to fall apart."

I nodded.

One night, Chad walked in on me sitting at the table, hunched over my math homework with a bowl of cereal that had gone soggy. He tossed his keys on the counter and said, "You good?"

I didn't look up. "Yeah. Just studying."

"You been studying every night like you about to cure cancer or something."

I didn't answer.

He pulled up a chair and sat across from me. "You don't talk to nobody anymore. You barely even come outside." "I'm just tired."

"Is it Jazz?" he asked. "I heard what she been saying." "I don't care about Jazz," I lied.

Chad shrugged. "You should. She jealous, and people like that stay mad when you don't stoop to their level."

"Why does she even care?" I said, finally meeting his eyes. "Why does everybody try so hard to break me?"

Chad didn't have an answer. He just sat there, silent.

"I didn't ask for any of this," I said, voice shaking. "Not Momma being locked up. Not moving from house to house. Not this life where I can't even breathe without being judged."

He leaned back, rubbing his chin. "You ever think maybe they mad 'cause you still shining?"

I scoffed. "What's shining about being on the struggle bus?"

"You still showing up; you still here. That counts."

That night, I cried into my pillow. Not because Chad's words fixed anything, but because I needed to. I needed to release the years of frustration now triggered by Jazz's actions.

The only place I let myself feel was when I got a letter from Momma. They felt like a church service. Her words reached into me and pulled out things I forgot I still felt.

"I'm so proud of you," she wrote. "Tell Bianca and Eric I love them with everything in me. You are my strength."

I would read her letter several times, let the ink blur from my tears, and for a moment feel love. No one said, "I love you, Jaydah." Not my family, at least. My family did acts of service, but I hadn't had anyone hug me, hold me, or tell me they loved me.

But by morning, the weight would return.

Jazz still found ways to whisper hate in the hallways.

Carmen still rolled her eyes at family gatherings, and even

Chad was funny acting sometimes.

One day, I caught Jazz outside, sitting on her porch, looking tired. She looked up at me but didn't say anything.

I surprised myself when I walked over.

"You good?" I asked.

She blinked at me. "Why you care?"

"I'm not tryna fight."

She laughed bitterly, "Since when do you even talk to people like me?"

I stood there, unsure of what to say.

She looked away. "People like you don't know what it's like to feel invisible."

That stopped me. I sat down on the edge of the porch.

"I feel invisible every day," I said. "I just learned how to fake like I'm not."

She didn't respond. But something in her eyes softened.

I didn't forgive her; it wasn't right then. But I understood something I hadn't before. Sometimes people hurt you because they're bleeding too.

LETTER FROM MOMMA

20 Feb 2000

Jaydah,

Hey, baby, I'll be glad to see you when I get home. I know that it was hard not to have me around for the Take Your Daughter to Work Day. For that, I'm sorry. I don't know if you remember, but we did that when you were younger and when I get home, we'll do it again. You keep your head up. Hope that granny brings you to see me soon. Love you, soul of my soul.

Luv

Mommie

CHAPTER 29

The Bruises You Can't See

I'd mastered the art of appearing fine. It was a skill, really. A polished surface, a practiced smile. I knew how to laugh at the right moments, how to show up to majorette practice with my hair slicked and my uniform crisp, how to answer "I'm good" even when my heart was caving in like a house on fire.

But I wasn't fine.

Not even close.

Six years had passed since Momma went to prison, and still there was no sign of her coming home. Granny was older now, slower on her feet, but she stayed committed. Every other month, she'd pile me, Bianca, and Eric into the car, gas up her beat-up sedan, and drive us halfway across the state just to sit behind a glass wall for forty-five minutes. Momma's smile never changed, but her voice was softer now. Like prison had taken some part of her spirit and refused to give it back.

That Texas heat always pressed down like it was trying to flatten us all. The pavement shimmered. The air conditioner at Granny's house clicked in and out. I'd lie awake most nights in the half-dark, wondering when this stretch of my life would end, wondering if I'd ever really start living, or if I'd just keep existing.

Tiff and Tamika kept me sane that year.

Tiff had a fire in her spirit that burned through every bad day. Her mom had just started a short bid for distribution charges, so Tiff was left to take care of her little brother, Marquise, by herself. I spent most of my summer helping her. We'd sit in her small kitchen, feeding him noodles while watching reruns on her cracked tablet, talking about everything and nothing. She never complained. She just handled it. Like me.

Tamika was the opposite, soft spoken, gentle like a whisper. She lived with two moms who loved her deeply but didn't always understand her. She was stuck in a toxic relationship with a boy who tore her down with words instead of fists. That was harder to explain to her moms. He made her feel small, and I recognized the signs – the way she flinched when her phone buzzed, how she cried when he didn't respond for hours, then crumbled when he finally did with a "You lucky I even talk to you."

"Why do you stay?" I asked one afternoon. We were walking home from the library, the sun melting into the pavement, our shadows long and quiet.

"I don't know," she whispered, staring at the ground.

"Because he sees me, I guess."

"No, he doesn't," I said. "He sees someone he can control.

That ain't love."

She didn't respond. Just kept walking.

That night, I wrote in my journal:

Dear Diary

Love shouldn't make you feel invisible. It shouldn't make you wait by the phone or wonder if you're enough.

I stared at those words until my eyes burned.

That night, I lay in bed and couldn't breathe. I had a dream Charles was standing over me, breathing heavily, eyes glazed like dirty glass. He didn't speak. He just stood there, a shadow in the doorway. When I jolted awake, I was shaking, the sheets soaked with sweat. I sat in the dark and asked myself a question I'd never dared to before: Did he touch me?

I didn't know. Maybe. Maybe not. But the fear I felt around him had never gone away. The memory of him hovering in doorways, too close. The way I always kept one foot pointed toward the exit, just in case.

That summer, I also found out what it meant to be violated in silence.

Tiff's cousin came down from Houston and stayed with us for a weekend. He was older, probably around twenty, but charming. Always smiling. The kind of man people trusted too quickly. One afternoon, I was sitting on the couch, folding laundry, when he sat next to me. Too close for my comfort. He asked me questions that felt too personal. When I stood up to leave, he grabbed my wrist.

"What's the rush, pretty girl?" he said, fingers tightening.

I pulled away, heart slamming against my ribs. "Don't touch me."

He smirked, leaned in closer. "You act like you don't like it."

When I tried to move past him, he blocked the door. Pinned me against it, pressing his head into my shoulder, breathing on my neck, touching places that weren't his to touch. I froze.

I didn't scream. I didn't tell. I just waited for it to be over.

Later, I told Tiff I didn't want to be around him. During a visit with her mom, she asked what happened. I told her he made me uncomfortable. She rolled her eyes and said, "Y'all young girls fast these days."

And that was that. I never went back.

I didn't talk about it. I couldn't. The world has already judged girls like me. Poor. Black. No daddy. A mom in prison. Who would believe I hadn't wanted it? Who would care?

I tucked the memory deep inside. Pretended it hadn't happened. But my body remembered.

At school, I wore extra layers even in the heat. I flinched when boys got too close. I stopped letting myself be alone with anyone I didn't trust.

Everyone else had plans for after high school. I had dreams, but no road map. Nobody sat me down and said, "Let's talk about applications." No one explained FAFSA or dorms or majors. I'd sit in the counselor's office alone, flipping through brochures and trying to imagine what college was like.

One day, I asked Granny, "Do you think I could go to college?"

She looked at me from her chair, eyes tired but steady.

"You can go wherever your faith take you."

"But what if my faith is tired?"

She reached for my hand. "Then let mine carry you." That stuck with me.

I thought about how fast Bianca and Eric were growing. I watched them and wondered if they could see the things I hid inside. The worry and the stress. I tried to smile when they needed joy. Tried to cook dinner like I wasn't exhausted. Tried to remind them they were loved, even when I didn't feel loved myself.

I thought back on a conversation I had with Bianca. She had crawled into my bed during one of our sleepovers at Granny's following a visit to see Momma.

"You think Momma's okay?" she asked, her voice tiny.

"Yeah," I said, stroking her hair. "She's okay. She loves you."

She paused. "Do you think she still loves herself?"

That question lodged in my chest. I didn't know the answer.

Sometimes I'd stand in the mirror and stare at my face.

Noticing how much I looked like Momma. Same eyes.

Same lips. Same fire. And I'd wonder, *is this my legacy?*

To survive what she survived? To endure what broke her and pretend I'm fine?

But other times, I believed I could be more.

I still danced. I still wrote in my journal. I still laughed with Tamika and Tiff, even through tears.

Coach pulled me aside after practice one day. Everyone else had cleared out, the gym quiet except for the squeak of her sneakers.

"You gonna let this world steal your shine?" she asked, arms crossed.

I shook my head, even though part of me wasn't sure.

She handed me a folded paper. A scholarship application. For girls like me, girls with grit, a story, and scars the helping hands placed along the way meant everything.

"I see you, Jaydah," she said. "Even when you're trying to disappear."

PART V

BECOMING MY OWN COVERING

Healing through memory, pain, and hope.

Chapter 30

Pieces of Her

The first day of senior year arrived. I was both excited and nervous. I walked through the double doors of the school I'd known for three long years, wondering if this place had ever really known me.

I never thought I'd make it this far, blending in with the other students despite my circumstances. I was the girl everyone admired but no one really understood. I was respected, liked even, but not truly known. And maybe that was on purpose. I had lived long enough behind masks to know being seen came with risks I wasn't always willing to take. When people saw too much, they started asking questions I didn't want to answer. I gave them what they needed to feel comfortable and kept the rest tucked safely inside.

The weight of almost finishing high school was heavy, and letters from Momma had begun to arrive more frequently. She'd started writing twice a month now, sometimes more. Each envelope carried words soaked in hope and apologies, stories from the inside and dreams of the outside.

"I'm proud of you, baby," she wrote in one letter. "Seven years down. Maybe one more to go if the parole board sees it in their heart."

One more year. The words rang in my mind like a chant and a warning. One more year until the world I'd been building without her would have to make space for her return. I wanted it desperately. And yet, I feared what it might undo. I feared how deeply I had buried my guilt, and what would happen when I had to face it.

Because I did blame myself.

Not in a dramatic, "it's all my fault" kind of way. But in the way a child does, quietly, inwardly, irrationally. I replayed those moments like scratched film in my mind: the day she left, the days before, the signs, the way I didn't ask enough questions, didn't beg her to stay, didn't scream loud enough to stop what was already coming. If I had done more, maybe she wouldn't have gotten in that car. Maybe the police wouldn't have stopped her. Maybe we wouldn't have fallen apart.

The weight of all that shaped me. I knew it. I could see how it carved lines into the way I loved people, with distance. It taught me to show up for others while rarely letting anyone show up for me. It made me shrink when I should have stepped forward. I turned self-sacrifice into a badge of honor instead of the bleeding wound it really was.

Tamika and Tiff started to notice too.

Tamika, with her soft eyes and voice like honey, had a tenderness that drew people in. Her life wasn't perfect, with a mother who worked two jobs and a stepmom with a habit of praising her one day and ignoring her the next, but she had structure, support, and a plan. She was headed to Prairie View A&M on a majorette scholarship. She'd known her college choice since sophomore year and had already auditioned and been accepted.

Tiff was the opposite. Wild-hearted and sharp-tongued, she moved through life with a hustle in her spirit. Her mom had just gone back to jail, again, and I found myself helping her watch her little brother most nights. We juggled diapers, homework, and dance practice as if we were mothers of three, instead of high school seniors. She never asked for sympathy; neither did I. That's why we got along so well.

Tamika was the dream. Tiff was the fight. I was stuck somewhere between them, trying to believe in something better, but unsure how to get there.

"I thought you were going to college," Tamika asked one afternoon as we lay stretched across her bedroom floor, homework scattered between us.

"I was," I said.

She turned to look at me. "Was?"

"I missed the audition deadlines. I didn't have anyone to help me with FAFSA. I don't even know where to start."

Tamika blinked slowly, processing. "You could've asked me."

"I know," I whispered, ashamed.

But the truth was, I was nervous about college. Everyone else had someone guiding them: parents, counselors, and mentors. The possibility of Momma coming home made the choice even harder. I needed to be in a place to support her when she returned, whether it be financially or emotionally.

That night, I went home to find a letter from Momma waiting on the kitchen counter. Granny had left it there next to a pot of beans still warm on the stove.

"I think they're serious this time," Momma wrote. "The parole board is reviewing everything. If it goes through, I could be home next Thanksgiving."

Thanksgiving. I read the word five times.

Could we really be whole again?

I didn't know how to answer that, and the guilt for not knowing was almost unbearable.

I wanted to give her everything she'd lost. I wanted to work, provide, and build a foundation she could come home to. That's when I made the decision to join the Army.

College felt too far away. Marriage was not an option. I liked Drake, the boy I had been seeing for a few months, but Granny's dreams of me becoming a church wife didn't align with my own. I didn't want someone to save me. I wanted to save us.

Drake and I met at a teen club on a Friday night. The lights were low, the music thumped through the floor, and the smell of sweat and cheap cologne filled the air. He was hard to miss, 6'2", caramel brown, solid in build like he was carved straight out of determination. A linebacker at his school, he moved with confidence but didn't brag. He asked me to dance, and we moved together like we'd known each other for years.

We exchanged numbers, and from there, it never slowed down. He was consistent. He called when he said he would, remembered what I told him, and actually listened. His grandmother was an evangelist, and that alone had Granny grinning ear to ear. "Now that's a boy raised right," she said the first time she met him.

Granny and his grandmother started calling each other, trading scriptures and recipes like they were already in-laws. Granny even joked about wedding colors one night. "I can see y'all in lavender and silver. Elegant, not too flashy," she said.

Drake would just laugh and play along, his arm wrapped around my shoulder. "As long as you walk down the aisle to my favorite song," he said, grinning.

"You don't have a favorite song," I teased.

"I will by then."

We weren't in love the way fairy tales tell it, but there was something real between us. He made me feel protected and treasured. I could be soft for once, without worry.

If Jazz hated me before, when she saw me with Drake, she hated me even more. She'd mutter things in the hallway and bump me at my locker. But I didn't care. It was that protection Drake exuded. When Jazz would come outside, barely dressed, Drake would be the one to say something to her and take my hand to walk off. I can remember him lifting me onto his shoulders like I was light as air, walking me to the corner store like I was royalty.

He and Chad even got along. Played Madden together like they were cousins.

Still, I was too young to marry anyone. I knew that, and deep down, so did Drake.

"Do what's best for you," he said when I told him about the Army. "We can make it work."

"I don't want to leave you," I admitted.

"But you will," he said. "And that's okay. Just don't lose yourself chasing what you think you owe everybody else."

His words stayed with me.

The Army promised stability, free college tuition, medical benefits, and a path forward. I needed all of it.

"Are you sure this is what you want?" Tamika asked again.

"You're so talented. You could dance professionally."

"I don't have time to chase dreams," I said. "I need something solid."

Tiff, always blunt, just said, "Do what you gotta do, J."

The night I signed my enlistment paperwork, I sat in the dark in our living room while the hum of late-night television filled the silence.

Chad was upstairs playing video games. Granny had gone to bed early. Aunt Dye was on a night shift. And Uncle Junior was, well, I wasn't sure. Some nights he was there, buzzing with energy and trying to fix the faucet that didn't need fixing. Other nights he disappeared for days and returned with tired eyes and trembling hands.

One morning, I walked into the kitchen half-asleep and froze.

The refrigerator was gone.

Not broken, not unplugged, gone.

Just a big empty square where it used to hum.

Uncle Junior was knocked out cold on the couch. Chad came bounding down the stairs, took one look, and yelled, "Where the hell is the fridge?!"

I smirked, already piecing it together. "Ask Uncle Junior."

By then, he was sitting up, scratching his head like nothing had happened. "I don't know. Somebody must've robbed us."

"Right," I said, with a smirk. "And they skipped the TV, Granny's china, and everything else."

Uncle Junior shrugged. "Maybe that's all they needed."

By sunset, the fridge was back, with no questions asked, and no explanation. Granny knew who Uncle Junior's dealer was and was usually able to pay whatever he owed to get back what he had traded for drugs.

That was how life was in that house, a wild story wrapped in silence. You just rolled with it, learned to laugh, and went on about your day.

One night, I sat on the porch with Granny. The air was heavy and quiet, perfect for reflection.

"You ever feel like you're carrying somebody else's life?" I asked.

She looked at me with serious eyes, then nodded slowly.

"Every damn day."

I looked at her, surprised.

"Don't mean I regret it," she added. "But it's necessary, just gets heavy sometimes."

I didn't say anything after that. I just sat there, letting her words settle into my bones.

I was beginning to understand I didn't have to carry everything all the time. Some burdens needed to be shed. I could let go of the guilt that didn't belong to me, could want something more for myself, even if it meant stepping away from what was expected.

My connection with Momma blurred her burdens into mine, like we were one. I needed to figure out the pieces of her from the pieces of me, and for the first time, I wanted to figure out where all my pieces belonged.

LETTER FROM MOMMA

9 Jun 2003

Jaydah,

Hey, Sweetie, got your letter. I was finally glad to hear from you, my red baby. How is everything going? How is your schooling? I know that you are happy to be done with basic training, and I'm proud of you, too. I am keeping the faith, Jaydah, you keep it, too. I'm so proud of ya'll babies. Ya'll have really grown up. We have a lot of catching up to do when I come home. I know you missed the mother-daughter stuff, but we have our whole lives to make up for it. I just wanted to tell you that I love you, soul of my soul.

Luv Mommi

CHAPTER 31

A Room of Her Own

The recruiter pulled up in an unmarked government van just after sunrise. I'd packed a small backpack the night before, taking what little I had. A few clothes, my government-issued paperwork, and the letter Momma sent last week, folded and worn from being read too many times. I stepped out onto the front porch of Granny's house one last time, hoping for someone, anyone, to say goodbye. Chad was asleep. Aunt Dye had worked the night shift and hadn't come home yet. Granny had said her goodbyes the night before in her own tired way, "Be safe, baby." Drake had to leave early for college to start football conditioning.

That morning, there was no send-off photo, no proud farewell. Just me standing in the wet hush of dawn with a buzzing knot in my stomach.

The recruiter, a broad-shouldered man in uniform, rolled down the window and gave a faint smile. "You ready?"

I nodded.

The drive to MEPS was quiet. He didn't talk much, just a few words here and there. For him, I was probably one of dozens this month. For me, it was everything.

At MEPS, we were processed quickly. Medical checks. More paperwork. Final signatures. A long wait in a cold room before boarding the flight to basic training. It was all a blur.

Basic training knocked the breath out of me. Not because of the running or the yelling or the early mornings, but because I had never lived with so many strangers before. Sixty women crammed into an open bay, with no privacy and barely any breathing room. Shower heads lined the walls, offering nothing but exposure. Every part of our day was regulated. When to eat, when to sleep, when to move. I found comfort in the predictability, even if it was suffocating.

The first week, I kept my head down, observed everything, and avoided trouble. There was a girl named Smith who cried every night into her pillow but still got up at 0430 sharp. Another, Private Lopez, cursed out the drill sergeant on day three and was gone by day four. There was no room for weakness or disrespect here.

I thought about Momma every time I laced up my boots. Every mile I ran, every blister I got, every punishment push-up, I thought about how she'd survived prison. If she could do years, I could do weeks.

I got a letter from Drake every week. Momma

"I'm proud of you," Momma wrote. "You're doing what I never got to. You're making a life for yourself. Keep going."

I read it again and again. Folded it and kept it in the inner pocket of my duffle bag.

Graduation came quicker than I expected. One minute I was shivering on the rifle range, the next I was marching across a parade field, sweat beading under my collar. The uniform felt stiff but powerful. For once, I wasn't pretending to be strong; I was strong.

When I saw Shay and Wendell in the crowd, holding Eric and Bianca between them, I nearly lost it. They waved, beaming. Bianca rushed into my arms after the ceremony, her voice loud and full of joy. "You look like a real soldier, Jaydah!"

That night, we stayed in a small hotel room off base. I slept beside them just like we used to when we were little, curled up, limbs tangled, like safety had come back in pieces. I didn't want morning to come.

But it did. And with it, orders to my first duty station.

The ride there was different. No fear this time. No doubt.

Just a strange calm.

At the base, I was greeted by PFC Johnson, a tall, no-nonsense woman with flawless skin and eyes that didn't miss a thing.

"This ain't basic anymore," she told me, handing over a small room key. "You're not in a cage. You're running your own life now. Don't screw it up."

She walked away before I could even thank her.

My dorm room was modest, with a twin bed; a simple desk, a closet, and a bathroom I didn't have to share. I turned the key and stepped inside. For a full minute, I didn't move. It was quiet. Clean. Mine.

No yelling. No cousins. No Granny. No side eyes from Aunt Dye. No arguments drifting from the kitchen. No slammed doors.

I let out a breath I hadn't realize I'd been holding.

That night, I unpacked everything slowly. I hung my uniforms with care, folded my civvies, arranged my small stash of books, and taped Momma's latest letter above the desk. I even opened the bathroom door twice just to admire the privacy.

Freedom tasted like stillness.

Within a few weeks, I'd settled in. I bought a used Corolla from a staff sergeant rotating out. I found a rhythm: PT in the mornings, duties during the day, downtime in the evenings. I'd call Bianca, Dee, and Eric sometimes, and check in with Momma through letters when I could. I wasn't far from home and visited Granny, Uncle Junior, and Aunt Dye often.

Drake and I would also meet up. His family adored me and welcomed me with open arms. I remember his baby cousins innocently quizzing me during a visit. We started to discuss marriage after he finished school.

One day, I received a text from an unknown number.

"I just want to let you know Drake has been coming to see me for several months and he has been getting money from me to spend on you."

"Who is this?"

"Alexis, we've been talking and hanging out for the past few months, and I just thought you should know."

"You can have him," I replied with anger.

I was not about to go back and forth with her. I sent Drake screenshots of her messages. He immediately called me.

"Baby, it's not like that," he pleaded.

"Drake, how does she even have my phone number? Do not lie to me."

There is nothing worse than a liar. Momma's voice in my head. She had told me a cheater could confess, a liar could return what they stole, but a liar, a liar could never be trusted.

"Jaydah, baby, just let me explain in person."

"Nah, Drake, I'm not stupid. That girl got my number out of your phone. Y'all were laid up. Yes, or no? Tell me now."

He called my name, followed by a long pause. "Yes, Jaydah. I've been kickin' it with her. She got mad because

I wouldn't leave you. She's just jealous. Don't let her break us apart."

"You broke us apart, not her."

My next visit home, I stopped to see his grandmother. She'd texted to check on me, and I promised to come by. I pulled up to his uncle's house. They had a two-story, six-bedroom home on an acre of land. His grandmother opened the door before I even had a chance to knock. I followed her into the dining room and sat with her.

"How have ya been, baby?" she asked.

"Good. I'm settling into the Army and getting ready to start school," I replied.

"I'm so happy to hear that," she said with a proud smile.

"How is Drake? Is he away at school right now?"

"Baby, Drake is in jail. He let his little friends get him caught up on a breaking and entering charge. He lost his scholarship and is in the county jail."

I was stunned. Drake, the same boy with dreams of the NFL and so much potential, had thrown it all away. She explained he was home on break when it happened, riding with some high school friends. They had him drive them to a house they planned to rob. He didn't go inside, but he was the getaway driver. That was enough.

We finished our conversation, and she walked me out to my car. She gave me a warm hug and whispered, "You're going places, baby. Leave him behind."

That night, I returned to my dorm, sat on the floor, stunned by Drake's actions, but also nervous about Momma's possible parole.

I needed to take my mind off the stress, so I cleaned my room top to bottom. Rearranged the closet. Organized my books. Changed the sheets. Lit the small lavender candle I'd hidden from inspection. And then I sat on the bed and breathed again.

Because I wasn't that girl who lost herself in the burdens of others anymore.

I had a room of my own. A key in my hand. A job. A future.

A voice.

And nobody - not Drake, not disappointment, not old pain - could take that from me.

CHAPTER 32

The Sound of Forgiveness

The fluorescent lights of the pediatric floor buzzed softly above my head as I finished restocking supplies for the shift. It had been a long day filled with tiny cries, cartoon voices on hospital TVs, and the metallic smell of antiseptic. I'd just wrapped up vitals check when my phone buzzed in my scrub pocket.

The number was unfamiliar but something in my spirit jolted.

"Hello?" I said, stepping into the supply closet for some privacy.

"Is this Jaydah?" the voice on the other end asked. It was warm, trembling, like it had been holding something in for too long.

"Yes, it is."

"This is the parole officer assigned to your mother's case. She's been approved for release. She'll be out next week."

The world around me slowed to a whisper. The shelves in front of me blurred. I couldn't breathe. Couldn't speak.

"Did… did you say next week?" I finally managed.

"Yes, ma'am. One week from today."

It wasn't a dream. It wasn't another letter about delays or hearings that led to nowhere. It was real. After eight years, eight years of steel doors and visiting rooms, of letters and longing—Momma was coming home.

I hung up the phone and slid to the floor right there in the closet. I didn't care if anyone walked in. The tears came hard, crashing through the steel wall I'd spent years building around my heart. I thought about the little girl who once cried herself to sleep, praying for her mother's return. I thought about the teenager who stopped hoping. The young woman who grew up too fast.

She was coming home.

The next seven days passed in a blur. I requested time off, packed a bag, filled the tank of my car, and prepared myself for something I wasn't sure how to feel about. Joy? Fear? Grief? All of it, maybe. Forgiveness was a sound I hadn't heard in years and I wasn't sure if I'd know how to say it aloud.

The day finally came. I made the four-hour drive back home in silence, the road humming beneath me like a lullaby. As I turned the final corner onto Aunt Shay's street, my palms began to sweat.

Then I saw her.

Standing in the front yard, arms outstretched, tears already falling.

I stopped the car, barely put it in park before I was out the door.

"Momma," I breathed.

She ran toward me, feet barely touching the ground, and we collided in an embrace so deep it felt like the ground shifted under us.

"I missed you so much," I sobbed into her shoulder.

"I never stopped missing you," she whispered, holding my face in her hands.

She looked older, lines etched deeper into her skin, her frame a little smaller, but her eyes were the same. Those same eyes that used to peek through cracked bedroom doors to check on us while we slept, that would sparkle when she sang to the radio while doing our hair. They were tired, but they were still Momma.

Inside, family came and went. Bianca was on her way. Eric had already seen her earlier that week. I sat on the couch watching them laugh, eat, talk about old times like they hadn't missed nearly a decade together. It felt like a dream I was too afraid to wake up from.

I kept my distance, not out of resentment, but reverence. I needed to absorb this. I needed to believe it.

Later, when it was just the two of us on the porch, I asked her why she didn't tell us she was up for parole.

"I couldn't stand the thought of y'all hoping again, just to be disappointed," she said, staring into the trees. "I needed to protect your hearts, even if it meant breaking mine."

That was Momma. Always protecting. Even from prison.

As the weeks went by, it became clear two grown women, both used to survival, both used to being right, couldn't coexist under one roof for long. Aunt Shay tried. She really did. But the unspoken resentments boiled over quickly. Words were exchanged, old wounds were poked.

"I took care of your damn kids for almost a decade," Aunt Shay hissed one night.

"And I thank you," Momma replied, her voice trembling.

"But you don't get to hold it over my head forever."

I watched the argument from the hallway, feeling the tension buzz like electricity.

That's when I made the decision.

I got a modest apartment just outside of town. It wasn't much, but it was clean and safe, enough room for Momma, Bianca, Eric, and a little peace. I signed the lease, paid the deposit, and helped them move in on a Saturday morning. I stood in the middle of the living room, looking around at the furniture we thrifted and borrowed, and for the first time in years, I felt like I'd given my mother something special: a place to start over.

A few weeks later, I got a call that shook my world again, but in a different way.

"Is this Jaydah?" the woman on the phone asked. Her voice was nervous, but kind.

"Yes?"

"My name is Gabby. I think I'm your sister." I sat down slowly. "My sister?"

"Your father's daughter. He… he told me about you years ago, and I've been looking for you since. I didn't know how to reach out."

My chest tightened.

I had a sister?

She was nearly 20 years older than me. Her life couldn't have been more different. Raised in California. Married. Two kids of her own. She told me our father was still alive, barely. He had congestive heart failure and his mother - my grandmother - was living too, but her health was fading.

We arranged a visit.

I stepped off the plane when a tall, slim, elderly man approached me with tears in his eyes.

"Jaydah, it's your daddy," his voice cracked.

He threw his arms around me as the tears flowed. A constant stream of apologies flowed from his lips. Sorry for leaving me, that I was always his little J.G, that he thought about me every day. I didn't have any anger or resentment in me. My sister and her children approached me and hugged me as well. It was awkward at first, strangers trying to build a bridge over decades of silence, but there was love still. An unexpected softness in the way my father looked at me, like I was still a baby.

I met my grandmother briefly. As soon as I walked in, she laid eyes on my face and said, "Yep, that's my granddaughter." She was fragile, her memory slipping in and out, but she held my hand and called me a "pretty girl." I met several aunts, uncles, cousins, nieces, nephews, and my older brother. It was a joyful experience my soul needed. I needed to fill that empty space and know the other side of my family. Not long after my visit, my grandmother passed away. Two months later, my father had a heart attack and died.

I cried at both funerals, not because I knew them deeply, but because I never got the chance. Grief is funny that way. It doesn't always wait for intimacy. Sometimes, it arrives simply because a door closed before you even realized it was open.

That year changed me.

I had been walking around for so long carrying pieces of other people, Momma's grief, my siblings' needs, my aunties' judgment. I never stopped to think about my own.

But watching Momma laugh again, helping Eric with homework, listening to Bianca dream about college – it reminded me why I kept going.

It reminded me why forgiveness matters.

Not just for them.

For me.

Forgiveness wasn't a loud declaration. It didn't happen all at once.

It sounded like silence after years of noise. It looked like letting Momma kiss my face after all these years. Like telling my father I love him after years of absence. Forgiveness is gentle, open, and graceful.

It was building trust in slow motion.

It was the sound of my heart learning how to beat without breaking.

CHAPTER 33

My Name is Jaydah

The morning sun poured through the window of my apartment, warm and golden like the promise of a new life. There was a peace in the way it stretched across the floor, falling softly on my white coat hanging by the door, pressed, pristine, ready. The gold embroidery stitched above the breast pocket shimmered slightly: Dr. Jaydah G. Olds.

I never got tired of reading that. Each time I saw it, I was reminded of how far I had come. I smiled as I ran my fingers across the lettering, tracing each letter like a prayer. Not for validation, but for reverence, for every version of me that never thought she'd get here.

The little girl who once sat in a food-stamp line with her head down.

The teenager who cried herself to sleep, wondering if her mother would ever come home.

The young woman who enlisted in the Army with trembling hands and dreams she was too afraid to speak aloud.

They were all still in me. But now, they had a new name, and it was mine.

"My name is Jaydah," I whispered to my reflection in the mirror.

It wasn't long after graduation that I bought Momma a new Sunday dress and took her to brunch. She looked radiant, stronger than she had in years. The dark circles under her eyes had faded. The tension in her shoulders had softened. And every time she reached across the table to touch my hand, it was like we were rebuilding brick by brick what time and circumstance tried to tear down.

"You're doing it," she said between bites of shrimp and grits. "Everything I prayed for… you're doing it."

"We're doing it," I corrected. "You kept going so I could, too."

She leaned back, tears pricking her eyes. "I thought I lost you."

"You did," I replied. "But we both found our way back."

Now, our family gathered every first Sunday. That was the rule. Sometimes it was brunch at Aunt Rita's house, sometimes it was lunch at a restaurant, but it always ended in laughter and leftovers.

Bianca was working at a local boutique, studying psychology part-time. She had the gentlest spirit, but don't cross her; she had Momma's fire in her.

Eric was growing into his own, all lanky limbs and mischief, the kind of teenager who thought he knew everything but still called me when he was sad and needed advice.

Dee had started flying home more often. He opened a luxury medical spa in Washington and sang in a jazz band on Friday nights. He still called me "Baby Doll," and he still gave the best hugs.

Granny had aged since Momma came home. Her steps were slower now. Her memory was sometimes fuzzy but her voice, her voice was still thunderous when she needed it to be.

When she passed away, we all wore white, just as she had requested. "No black at my funeral," she had said with a wink. "Y'all better celebrate me like I made it."

We did.

We filled the church with music and food and stories. I delivered the eulogy, my hands trembling as I looked out at a sea of faces, each one touched by the woman who raised so many.

"She taught me how to fight," I said from the pulpit, my voice cracking. "But more than that, she taught me how to forgive and because of her, I no longer run from my story. I walk in it."

A few weeks later, I was on a panel at a medical conference when one of the attendees asked about my background.

"Where are you from?" she asked.

I smiled. "I'm from a place most people run from. But I didn't. I leaned into it. My mom was incarcerated when I was a child. My grandmother raised me in a home filled with struggle, love, and sacrifice. I joined the Army to survive. I became a doctor because I wanted to thrive. My name is Jaydah. And my story doesn't begin with perfection, but it ends with purpose."

The room went quiet. Then, applause.

One night after work, I sat with Momma on the back balcony of her apartment, Bianca was inside making dinner, and Eric had just come home from football practice.

"You ever think about those early years?" she asked, lighting a cigarette.

"Sometimes," I said. "But not like I used to."

"How do you forgive someone who couldn't protect you?"

I looked at her. The same question had once kept me up at night.

"I realized," I said slowly, "that forgiveness isn't about forgetting what happened. It's about making peace with it. I forgave you because I needed to be free, and I knew you were already carrying enough. Momma, nobody's perfect."

Momma blinked. Her eyes shone in the porchlight. She flicked ash from her cigarette and nodded. "Thank you for not giving up on me."

"I couldn't," I said. "You're my mother."

I wasn't the same girl anymore. I didn't flinch at backhanded comments or fold under pressure. I walked into rooms like I belonged there, because I did.

I had learned how to be soft without being weak. How to love without disappearing. How to lead without carrying anyone's burden but my own.

CHAPTER 34

Soul of My Soul

The scissors clicked rhythmically, their metallic slice cutting through the low bustle of conversation like a pulse. Hair dryers roared in the background, layered beneath the soothing melodies of 90s soul drifting through hidden speakers. The familiar scent of freshly flat-ironed hair mixed with the calming undertone of eucalyptus oil lingered in the air, grounding every breath. Back Rooted Beauty Bar & Spa was more than a business now; it was a sanctuary. It pulsed with life, resilience, and Black womanhood reimagined.

Bianca stood near the front desk, greeting clients with her signature warm smile and quick wit, her hair tied up in a silk scarf. She moved with confidence between reception and her massage suite, shoulders relaxed, voice smooth. Her healing hands had become just as requested as Momma's. Watching her now, you wouldn't guess the years of uncertainty we both carried on our backs. She glowed with purpose.

Momma was in the styling room, pressing out a young girl's hair while giving life advice in between gentle strokes. She was in her element. Her hands moved with grace and precision, trained not just by cosmetology school but through years of survival, healing, and growth. Her voice was low and patient, the kind that made people lean in. It wasn't just the style they came for; it was the soul work.

From the window of my upstairs office, I looked out over the block. The sign for Eric's barbershop gleamed across the street, packed with loud talking and laughing. He'd learned from the best, watched old heads in neighborhood shops, and added his own twist. His lineups were clean, fades so sharp they felt spiritual. But it was more than skill. Eric had a way of talking to boys, ones who didn't like to talk. He taught them dignity with every edge-up, patience with every brush of the clippers.

Inside my office, the sun caught the glass frame on the wall and my medical school diploma, still surreal, Jaydah G. Olds, M.D. I had earned every letter. Not to prove anything to anyone, but because I knew what it meant to fight for your own voice in a world that tried to silence you. Against every statistic, every snide remark, every institutional obstacle, I had made it. And even more than that, I had brought my people with me.

The door creaked behind me. I didn't have to turn to know who it was.

"You ready?" Bianca asked, voice soft and sacred, as if she didn't want to disturb the moment too loudly.

I turned to face her. "I'm ready."

She grinned and stepped inside, helping me adjust the white satin dress I wore for the pre-ceremony moments. It wasn't the wedding gown yet, just something simple and elegant to hold the quiet reverence of the morning.

We walked down the back steps and into the limousine, where Momma was already waiting. Her eyes welled with tears the moment she saw me and I let myself be held, rocked for just a moment in the arms that had seen me through everything.

The venue was tucked away in a garden just outside the city, a hidden gem surrounded by ancient oaks and whispering wind. Eric stood near the entrance, checking to make sure everything ran on time.

"Can't let the groom see you yet," he joked, throwing me a knowing smile. "It's bad luck."

We slipped into the bridal suite. Tamika was already there, my Matron of Honor, carefully laying out the gown. Tiff, my Maid of Honor, fussed over the shoes and jewelry.

The dress was everything. Off-the -shoulder, mermaid style, white tulle flowing like water behind me. As Bianca laid the train across the floor, Momma stepped back and let out a soft breath.

"You look just like I dreamed," she said.

I smiled through the tears rising in my throat. "No, Momma. I look exactly how you made me."

Outside, soft music floated through the trees. The ceremony was about to begin.

We kept it small on purpose, fifty guests, all family by blood or soul. Everyone wore white or cream, a nod to Granny's memorial, where we'd honored her life in the same colors. This time, it wasn't for mourning. It was for resurrection.

Dee stood at the aisle's start, his suit perfectly tailored, the silver in his beard catching the sunlight. He looked peaceful, whole.

"You ready, baby girl?" he asked, holding out his arm.

"I've been ready my whole life," I said.

The doors opened. India Arie's *"I am ready for love"* played softly from a string quartet under a white canopy. The aisle was lined with flower petals, roses, gardenias, and calla lilies, each one hand-laid that morning by my nieces and Bianca's best friend's daughters.

And there was Jahlil.

He stood tall at the altar, dressed in a cream suit that glowed against his deep brown skin. His gold cufflinks shimmered, and his beard was freshly lined. His eyes locked onto mine and the way he smiled, it was like he saw me—not just the bride, but the woman beneath every layer of healing and hope.

We'd met two years ago through a friend from med school. I hadn't planned to fall in love; I was too busy rebuilding. But Jahlil was different. A trauma surgeon with a quiet strength, a heart scarred by his own childhood, yet somehow more open than anyone I'd ever met.

He saw me. Not just the polished, public me, but the parts I tried to keep hidden.

"I see your bruises," he told me once after I cried during a documentary about incarcerated women. "But I see your brilliance more."

As I walked toward him, I felt light. Not weightless, but carried.

The ceremony moved like a sacred rhythm. Vows exchanged beneath the trees. Tears and laughter folded into each word. When the officiant asked, "Who gives this woman to be married today?" Dee stepped forward, voice steady.

"I do."

Momma's voice followed from the front row, thick with emotion. "She carries the soul of my soul."

After the ceremony, we danced under the stars, barefoot on the grass. Bianca gave a toast that turned into a tribute.

"To my sister," she said, holding her glass high. "You held it down when nobody saw you. You gave me safety. You gave us all love."

Eric teased me about my childhood obsession with organizing everything, "She even had her dolls marching in formation!" and everyone laughed.

Jahlil held me close for our first dance, the music low and slow.

"Thank you," I whispered into his chest.

"For what?" he murmured.

"For choosing me. For not being afraid of my scars."

He kissed the top of my head. "My Lioness. I didn't just choose you, Jaydah. I recognized you. You built a whole kingdom from scraps. I'm just lucky I get to build with you."

Later that night, the crowd thinned. Candles flickered in glass jars. The DJ played our last song. One by one, guests disappeared into the night, leaving only the echoes of celebration behind.

We entered our honeymoon suite, laughter still caught in our throats. I slipped out of my dress, wiped away the last of my makeup, and stood barefoot on the balcony.

Below, the city lights pulsed in the distance, and a soft wind curled through the air.

I closed my eyes, letting the silence hold me.

Momma was thriving now, mentoring paroled women. Bianca was taking business classes and discussing franchising. Eric had signed the lease for a second barbershop. Dee was moving to Spain to teach. Our family, once fractured, had become a constellation.

I whispered into the night: "My name is Jaydah G. Olds-Harper. I am the daughter of a woman once bound but never broken. The granddaughter of wisdom and strength, the sister of warriors, the wife of a King, and I carry the soul of every girl who thought she'd never make it."

Above me, the stars didn't speak.

But I felt the peace of their presence; a familiar, bright, translucent blur floated over them.

It was then I understood I had never been alone.

www.ingramcontent.com/pod-product-compliance
Lightning Source LLC
LaVergne TN
LVHW041200150826
845673LV00001B/231

* 9 7 9 8 9 8 8 8 7 1 6 9 9 *